MW00931648

dixi
books

Moyra Irving

Moyra Irving is a writer, storyteller, and Creative Writing teacher who lives in Central England.

Her writing career began with a collection of short stories, one of which led to the creation of The Extra Guest end-hunger charity which is partnered with Oxfam and SOS Children's Villages.

She has also published two non-fiction books: *Take Me to the Mountain* and *Fiery Love*. However, it wasn't until *Amelie Trott* came into her life that she discovered the unparalleled joy of writing for children.

Moyra also loves cats, starry nights, days by the sea and, more than anything, writing stories for the child in us all.

This is her debut children's novel.

Amelie Trott & The Earth Watchers

Moyra Irving

Dixi Books

Copyright © 2020 by Moyra Irving

Copyright © 2020 Dixi Books

All rights reserved. No part of this book may be used or reproduced or transmitted to any form or by any means, electronic or mechanical, including photocopying, recording, or by any information and retrieval system, without written permission from the Publisher.

Amelie Trott and The Earth Watchers

Moyra Irving

Editor: Andrea Bailey

Designer: Pablo Ulyanov

Cover Design: Barrie Eyden

I. Edition: March 2020

Library of Congress Cataloging-in-Publication Data

Moyra Irving - 1st ed.

ISBN: 978-619-7458-94-7

1. Ecology 2. Middle Grade Fiction 3. Environmental Fiction
4. Fiction About Values & Virtues for Children 5. Children's Friendship
6. Children's Action and Adventure

© Dixi Books Publishing

20-22 Wenlock Road, London, England, N1 7GU

info@dixibooks.com

www.dixibooks.com

Amelie Trott & The Earth Watchers

Moyra Irving

dixi
books

The Voice of the New Age

For Amelie, my best little friend

Acknowledgements

My heartfelt thanks go firstly to Ayse Ozden at Dixi Books for allowing Amelie to fly!

My love and gratitude go also to Alorah Parks for her invaluable guidance and inspiration; to my wonderful son John-Patrick for his honest appraisal; and to Ali cat, my precious little muse.

Thanks to author Keith Forrest and all my treasured friends for their active involvement and encouragement - too many to mention but I hope you will know who you are. You have all helped to make this book a reality.

A special tribute also to my friend, the late singer-songwriter Mel Ellis, for her beautiful lyrics, 'Peace Begins with Me' (Chapter 33), and to Barrie Eyden who brought my characters to life in his magnificent cover art.

Next, I must honour my first young reader, Tabitha Wilson. Though we have never met, Tabby kindly agreed to assess the very first draft and wrote me the most beautiful review. She has definitely earned a place in my next novel!

I shall never forget the teachers and children of St. Mary's Catholic Primary School in Newcastle-under-Lyme who invited me to pilot my book and whose wonderful enthusiasm spurred me on in my search for a publisher. Thank you all!

Finally, to the one at my shoulder, urging me on: I know you are there.

Chapter One

August 2018: The Story That Won't Go Away

'So, Amelie,' the reporter began with a smirk, 'when did you first meet these, er… little green men?'

A murmur of laughter rippled through the hall and Amelie Trott, aged ten years and eleven months, rose to her feet. 'Kindly don't insult my intelligence!' she replied, eyeing him sternly. 'Don't forget, these are my friends…'

A tiny figure amidst the gaggle of newsmen and women, she commanded immediate attention, not least for her bright poppy-red hair caught in little bunches at the side of her head. 'They deserve our utmost respect. And remember,' she said, her eyes still fixed on the errant reporter: 'Earth Watchers are a civilisation far more advanced than our own.' And as she spoke she appeared to grow taller, more radiant, as though lit from within by a thousand suns. She shone like a beacon at sea.

Five hundred journalists looked on, mystified; some shifted in their seats, others scribbled in notepads. Was this really the voice of a ten-year-old girl?

'Is it true they're abducting people?' one asked.

'Not entirely…' Her sombre young face broke into a mischievous smile. 'However,' she added, amused by some private thought, 'there is one case I know of; let's just say, someone who needed to be taught a lesson.'

A woman in a snazzy red suit leapt up from her seat. 'May Curley, Sky News… Those lights we saw in the sky, are you really telling us they're *aliens*?'

Amelie's green eyes flashed. 'Aliens? No, Ms. Curley, I'm not, so kindly don't use that word! And may I suggest you watch my video on YouTube? Next question, please…'

'Jeremy Loudly, BBC News. Only ten years old and here you are, addressing this International Press Conference.' He paused to brush a stray tear from his eye. 'You've already written a book, organised a global campaign, and now have the world at your feet… How on earth did that happen? And what would you say to other aspiring young children like yourself?'

'Just this…' she said gently and the light in the centre of her chest glowed. 'You can achieve absolutely anything if you remember this one thing:

There is an amazing Invisible Power running through each one of us…' She glanced around at the surprised faces before her, her voice clear as a bell. 'Yes, through you too… You are never too small, too young, or too old to make a difference.'

'So, what's next then, Amelie? Any more missions planned?'

She smiled mysteriously. 'Oh yes, there's still much to be done. The adults of the world can no longer be trusted to safeguard the future of our planet. You see, Jeremy, this is a story that won't go away…'

Chapter Two

July 2018: The Approaching Storm

Two small figures, a boy and a girl, raced through the rain-soaked streets that morning. 'Amelie!' the boy shouted over his shoulder, 'we're late now, all thanks to you!' He jumped the puddles with ease, zig-zagged his way deftly between cyclists and pushchairs.

Way behind him his mud-splattered sister was struggling to keep up. 'Sorry!' she gasped, dodging in vain the spray of a passing car. 'I had to go back for my lucky rainbow pen. Not that it's brought me much luck so far today. Mum says we're going to be homeless…'

As they neared the school gates Tim paused briefly to catch his breath. 'Homeless? What on earth do you mean?'

'I heard her talking to Dad.'

Tim dug his hands in his pockets. 'Dad's dead,' he said flatly. 'You can't talk to dead people.'

'Well, Mum does.' Amelie stared him out defiantly, her wild red hair caught by the wind. 'She told him our house is falling apart and we'll finally be *detsachute*…'

'Destitute,' Tim corrected, climbing the steps ahead of her.

'That's what I said.' She pictured them both, huddled together in some draughty shop doorway with only their woolly hats and sleeping bags for comfort, while her tears fell unnoticed in the rain. 'I don't know how I'll get through today,' she said dramatically, clutching his arm.

'Don't worry, there's always the old playhouse,' Tim joked, shouldering his sister through the main door. 'Or my tent...' He grinned but his mind was racing. 'No way are we losing Hadleigh House. Anyway,' he added sensibly, 'we can't do anything now. Why don't you talk to your friends?'

'What friends?' she snapped. 'They all think I'm mad. You know I've only got Storm and Isla. And you, I suppose.'

'At least you've got Maths,' he said, suppressing a smile. 'That'll take your mind off things for a bit.'

'I hate you,' Amelie said, shaking her umbrella in his face.

The rain continued and by afternoon purple clouds had gathered and the first rumble of thunder heralded the approaching storm. Amelie wriggled uncomfortably, her feet still damp from the puddles.

Miss Snarkey, head teacher of Havenbridge School, swept into the room and greeted her class with an armful of end-of-year test papers and a malevolent stare.

Amelie shrank back in her seat and clutched her lucky rainbow pen. How wonderful, she thought, to be invisible at will!

'Amelie Trott, make yourself useful for once and give these out...'

Amelie stifled a yawn and glared at the old black clock on the wall, willing its stiff little hands to move: *Tock! Tock!*

'Get a move on then, girl!'

'Okay, okay...' She scrambled out of her seat, scraping her shin on the table leg.

When she returned to her place by the window she was surprised to see an unfamiliar boy already seated at the table beside her. 'Fractions and decimals!' she groaned, nursing her bruised shin. She handed him the last of the test papers. 'You might as well have this as I haven't a clue.'

He glanced at it briefly and laughed. 'Hah! That's-easy-enough...'

Amelie watched in surprise as he filled the page with neat little squiggles. 'There-job-done!' he said, pretending to dust off his hands. 'Go-on-then-write-your-name-at-the-top.'

Amelie frowned. Judging by the way he spoke he wasn't from around here. But there was something else about him, a brightness that made everything else look dull. Which of course it was, she sighed, her eyes drawn back to the old black clock on the wall. Its hands definitely hadn't moved since the last time she'd checked. 'Hey, you did that in no time at all!'

'That's-right,' he said in his strange mechanical voice. 'No-time-at-all...'

'My great-grandfather's ridiculously clever too,' Amelie said earnestly, looking out at the rain and the trees, buffeted by the squall. 'His name is Storm. He entered the world on a wild and blustery night ninety-four summers ago when the streets were full of horse-drawn carts and gas lamps, and everyone wore hats...'

'Wow...!' The boy began to clap. 'That's-pretty-cool-you-know!'

Amelie eyed him, half-curious; what a funny kid he was with his big round eyes, and unusually large hands. Weird too him turning up here on the last day of term... 'You see,' she whispered, aware of the head teacher's warning scowl, 'his first cry was so *thunderous* it woke all the servants and frightened the dogs.'

'You-really-*must*-write-a-book.' His face shone like it was lit by a hundred watt bulb.

'Maybe,' she grinned. 'I'm pretty rubbish at everything else...'

'You-can-tell-a-great-story-though...' When he smiled it was as though he'd switched on a lamp in the centre of his chest, all orange-gold like a flame.

Amelie frowned. 'Did you really mean it, about the book?'

'Of-course! Amelie-Trott-best-selling-author…'

A sly Voice of Doubt harrumphed inside her head. *Best-selling author? You can't even spell!*

'Take-no-notice,' the boy laughed, just as though he had heard her thoughts.

Her small, freckled face shone with pleasure. Suddenly, sleeping in doorways no longer seemed to matter so much. 'Then I suppose I'd better get used to signing my name,' she said lightly. She picked up her pen, filled it with rainbow ink and carefully wrote her name.

Amelie J. Trott

BEST-SELLING ~~AUTHER~~ AUTHOR

'Now-make-it--a-bit-more-flamboyant…'

'More eye-catching, you mean? I will…' She nodded and placed a small star over the 'i' in place of a dot and crossed the 't's with spirals like tangled string. 'How's that?' Laughing, she spun round to show him.

'Talking to chairs now are we, Miss Trott?' Miss Snarkey lowered her spectacles and viewed her suspiciously. 'Perhaps you'd care to share with the class, hmm?'

Amelie frowned at the empty chair beside her. 'Where is he, Miss Snarkey, that new kid next to me?'

'New kid?' Miss Snarkey sighed irritably. 'Don't be ridiculous! There's no one next to you, nor will there be. You have thirty minutes to finish. Stop mind-wandering, girl, and get on with your work!'

Bewildered, Amelie propped her chin in her hands and gazed wistfully into the distance. In her mind she was already home; warm and dry in their big, steamy kitchen where the sweet smell of baking pervaded the air. Not that this was very likely today with Mum so upset about the house. She lingered there awhile like a hungry ghost before drifting into the cool, tiled hallway that led to Great-Grandfather Storm's private study: the perfect place for a mind-wander.

William Storm Trott, whose turbulent nature lived up to his name, knew everything from the capital city of Madagascar to who had won the 1938 FIFA World Cup, and a great deal more besides. He could even count up to one hundred in Tibetan and was a firm believer that mind-wandering was the greatest of human gifts since it had the potential to *unlock doors to hidden worlds*. And Amelie was about to find out just how true this actually was...

Chapter Three

The Perfect Place for a Mind-Wander

Amelie stood at the open door, breathing in the delicious scent of lavender polish and old leather-bound books. Tiptoeing inside, she perched on Grandpa Storm's big swivel chair, and began to whirl; so fast that the earth spun around her and the dismal old schoolroom soon ceased to exist.

At last, she came to a halt and indicated a thick pile of papers on Storm's desk. 'Wake up, Freddie!' she cried to a sleepy black cat on her lap. 'I've written you a story...'

Hearing his name, the little cat pricked up his ears and yawned. Amelie patted his head then curled her hands around a steaming mug of hot chocolate that had conveniently placed itself before her. It was heaped with marshmallows and frothy whipped cream, essential additions to any good mind-wander. The cat blinked amiably and pounced on the papers, batted them with his paw and sent them scattering onto the floor. She was about to reproach him when a sudden noise took her attention and she glanced up to find someone clambering in through the open window.

'Oh, it's you again,' she laughed, 'the new kid from school!'

'Yes-I'm-Dorin,' he replied in his funny, mechanical way. He promptly gathered up her papers, shuffled them as skilfully as a magician with a pack of cards and, with a flick of his wrist, replaced them with a beautifully bound paperback book. He waved it under her nose. 'Come-along-there's-no-time-to-lose…'

'Excuse me,' Amelie interrupted, spilling most of the chocolate down her front, 'I may be mind-wandering but how on earth did you do that?'

'Hurry!' he ordered sharply, dismissing her question, 'they-are-waiting.'

'Waiting?' she puzzled. 'Who's waiting?' But he had already grasped her wrist and was pulling her to her feet. Very soon they were flying out of the window and down the hill, Dorin still clutching the book and their feet barely touching the ground. They wove their way swiftly through narrow streets bustling with Friday shoppers, and finally came to a halt outside a tall half-timbered building.

'Bookland!' Dorin announced with an elaborate bow and the light at the centre of his chest glowed. 'It's-your-big-day-Amelie-Trott…'

Was this really happening, she wondered? It certainly felt like it was. There was even a little red mark on her wrist where Dorin had gripped her. Nervously, she looked around her. Bookland was packed with noisy, jostling children; reporters hovered and cameras flashed. And wherever she turned, there were photographs smiling back at her; a girl with freckles and poppy-red hair in little bunches at the side of her head. 'Is that really me, Dorin?' she whispered.

'Of-course!' He dragged her towards a large display stand at the front of the store, piled high with colourful paperbacks. 'But-it's-a-future-you. You-see?' He added her book to the pile. 'Your-latest-literary-success!'

More than curious, Amelie glanced at its cover. There was her name, *Amelie J. Trott*, and below it in large, gold embossed letters:

THE EXTRAORDINARY ADVENTURES OF WILD BILLY STORM

In your dreams, snorted the Voice of Doubt, *only clever people write books!*

Amelie returned to her desk with a jolt. 'Stop that at once,' she commanded, 'you're boring me now...' She looked down in surprise at the chocolatey stain on her dress and the little red mark on her wrist.

'Boring you? Insolent child!' Miss Snarkey twitched her beak-like nose. 'Chop! Chop! All work to the front...' but her words were soon lost in the *brrring* of the bell and the great clatter of chairs that signalled the end of the day.

Amelie leapt to her feet, flung her schoolbag over one shoulder and joined the surge of children hurrying towards the door.

'Not so fast, Miss Trott!' Miss Snarkey held Amelie's test paper between her finger and thumb as though it had just fallen in something horribly smelly and unhygienic. 'What's this nonsense anyway?' she asked ungraciously, taken aback by the girl's inexplicably perfect work. A blob of spit landed on Amelie's chin which she quickly wiped away with her sleeve. 'This here: *best-selling author?*' Two angry red spots appeared on her face.

'Oh, that. I'm writing a book, Miss Snarkey.'

'Book!' The head teacher bared her big yellow teeth. 'Really, my dear?' she enquired nastily. 'You mean there's actually something between your ears, hmm?' She peered at Amelie over her spectacles. 'Your work this year has been nothing short of atrocious. And as for your end of year report! I shall be posting that to your mother myself and spend the next six weeks considering further action...'

The sky was still heavy with rain and Amelie paused to put up her umbrella before racing down the steps to join her brother.

Tim was waiting under the trees at the end of the long school drive. 'Whatever kept you?' he grumbled. 'I'm getting soaked here.'

'Snarkey,' Amelie panted, offering her umbrella. 'Here, share this.'

'On the last day of term? That's a violation of human rights.'

'Violetation...?'

'Violation,' Tim corrected, 'you know, it's like she's breaking the law. She has to go. Hey, why don't we start a petition...?'

'Or a demonstration...' Amelie's green eyes glistened. She could already see banners and TV cameras, microphones, even interviews on the Six O'clock News with World Affairs correspondent, Jeremy Loudly. 'And take it to the Town Hall, or better still the Prime Minister. Get Snarkey Out!'

'Careful!' Tim warned, walking more quickly. 'Here come the Specks... Let's hope they didn't hear.'

Twins Jonathan and Felicity Speck in Year Nine were Miss Snarkey's Secret Agents. They spoke to each other out of the corner of their mouths and had a very nasty habit of sneaking up on you whenever you least suspected.

Amelie pulled a face. 'By the look on their smug little faces they just did. As though I'm not in enough trouble already...'

'Have you got your report?'

'Snarkey's posting it. It's *astroshus*.'

Tim smiled. 'So, what's new?'

'Further action, whatever that might mean. Anyway,' she continued, 'I must tell you this. There was this new kid today who did my test for me and said I must write a book...'

Yeah, yeah, murmured the sly Voice of Doubt.

'I'll show you!' she shouted and Tim stared at her, bewildered. 'Anyway, he said I'd be a best-selling author...' She stopped there, seeing the look on his face.

'What a weird thing to say.'

'I know. But then, I thought, if I really was it might be a way to save our house...'

'Really?' Tim snorted, accustomed to his sister's funny ideas. 'I don't think so.' He stopped walking and dragged a very battered old volume out of his bag. 'Talking of books, Flakey let us read instead of Maths.'

Amelie pictured nice Mr Cornthwaite, telling them jokes with his feet on the desk and a big sleepy grin on his face. Cornflake, they called him though this was often shortened to Flakey because he was pleasantly odd, with sticky-up hair and crumpled clothes that made him look rather like an unmade bed.

'Okay for some,' she snapped, storming on ahead with her umbrella. 'Some of us had to work. Except, I didn't, of course,' she added with disarming honesty.

'Look,' Tim said, clutching *The Hornby Dublo Book of Trains*, 'I've had an idea: a kind of futuristic model railway...'

'Awesome,' Amelie said, faking a yawn.

'We'd charge people loads to see it...'

'Model railway?' Amelie shot him a look of despair. 'How boring is that? What's up with you, Tim? You're stuck in a time-warp. All you need is an old school cap and a pocket full of conkers.'

'Modern, high-speed flying trains, you bozo! I'm reviving an old family hobby with state-of-the art technology. Storm lent me this as well.' He searched in his bag and produced a small leather notebook. 'Storm's diary from when he was my age. There's even an inscription inside: *The Extraordinary Adventures of Wild Billy Storm...*'

Amelie froze. 'Did you say Wild Billy Storm?' she gasped. 'But that's the title of my best-selling book!'

Chapter Four

The Curious Appearance of the Ten Foot Tall Man

'You'll have to ask Storm,' Tim said firmly. 'You can't just write a book about someone without telling them.'

'Well, that's a pity.' Amelie said, struggling to stop her umbrella from turning inside out, 'I really want it to be a surprise.'

Battered by wind and rain, they hurried through the little town until they came at last to Cloud Hill. At the very top, and exposed to the elements, stood Hadleigh House. Once a fine Victorian manor, it had been home to the Trott family since the late 1800s and now belonged to their mother, local artist Lucy Elizabeth Trott. Sadly, the old house had grown rather shabby over time, with flaking paintwork and crumbling bricks. Draughts sought out gaps under doors and rattled window panes; high winds dislodged tiles on the roof.

There were many legends surrounding the little seaside resort of Havenbridge, but none were as strange as the mystery of Hadleigh. Here, it was rumoured, were underground tunnels where smugglers once stored gold; and a miraculous Stone of Power that promised wealth and success for its keeper.

'Stones with magical powers?'

'Nah, the Trotts are poor as church mice. Not a penny to their name...'

But there were those who knew its secrets and were determined to banish the Trotts as fast as they could.

Tim and Amelie trudged up the drive and arrived at the back of the house. 'I do hope Mum's all right,' Amelie said, scraping mud off her shoes on the step. 'I've been worrying about her all day.' She flung open the kitchen door and a warm, comforting smell of baking greeted them, suggesting that maybe things weren't so bad after all.

'Yay! Chocolate fudge cake! Thanks Mum,' Amelie said, observing her mother closely. 'Everything okay?'

Lucy Trott looked up from mopping the floor and smiled. 'Apart from a flood in the attic...'

'Oh.' Amelie shook her umbrella in the doorway and dumped her schoolbag on the table. 'Well, I've got something really important to do before Isla arrives,' she announced briskly before her mother could ask any awkward questions concerning reports. 'I'm writing a book.'

'Hey, just a minute, young lady...' Lucy commanded, surveying the trail of puddles behind them. 'Take off those wet things first. We don't want a flood in here too. Oh, and before I forget...' Her voice suddenly became suspiciously bright. 'Cousin Magnus is coming to tea.'

'Magnus!' Tim rolled his eyes. 'Cheers, Mum, but why?'

'Because I phoned Mona about the roof...'

'Yeah, like Auntie Mona knows anything about roofs!'

'No, but Uncle Maynard does and being in the property business he's pulled a few strings. He's found a roof man for us, a Mr Dankstone...'

'Really?' Amelie said scornfully. 'Since when did that lot ever do anything for us?'

'Well...' she consoled, 'it's only for a couple of hours and the lovely Isla will be here too, remember.'

Amelie warmed her hands by the stove. 'I suppose,' she relented, cheered by the thought of Isla's visit. 'As long as he doesn't eat all the cake; you know what he's like.'

'Anyway,' Lucy said, pulling on her artist's smock, 'I have a lot of work to do in the studio. Will one of you let Mr Dankstone in? Yes, and do be nice. He may be our only chance of saving the house. And Amelie, keep an eye on the cake; it'll be ready in twenty minutes. Here, Tim, you take this bucket up to the attic to catch the drips…And don't disturb Storm, either of you, he's asleep.'

Grudgingly, Tim disappeared with the bucket and his *Hornby Dublo Book of Trains.* 'Then I'm building Havenbridge Junction so don't anyone dare disturb *me* either,' he said, looking pointedly at his sister. The door slammed loudly behind him.

'Nerd,' Amelie muttered; a word she had learned from Tim. She opened her bag and ripped a page out of her school planner. She rummaged around in the kitchen drawers for some Blu Tack and the largest felt-tipped pen she could find and wrote on it in large letters: NOVELL IN PROGRES DO NOT DISTERB. She held it up proudly to show her mother who wondered if her little daughter would ever learn to spell.

Lucy looked out at the rain. There would certainly be no holidays in the sun for the Trotts this year; and the thought of six weeks with two bored children under her feet did little to raise her spirits, not to mention the roof. Just as well Tim had the old train set to occupy him. But Amelie *writing a book* - wherever did she get these crazy ideas?

'Please don't forget that cake,' she repeated loudly.

Amelie nodded. 'But first I must find my special notebook; the one Storm gave me for Christmas.'

'You must let me read your book when it's finished.'

'Don't worry, I will.' Amelie sauntered off, clutching her hand-written sign and a piece of Blu Tack rolled into a ball. 'It's about Storm,' she added as an afterthought. 'You can design the cover if you like.'

She found the little notebook in a drawer in her bedroom,

still wrapped in its Christmas paper. She tucked it under her arm and hurried downstairs. Halfway down, she stopped and squatted on the worn stair carpet. Out of all the wonderful nooks and crannies in the old house, this was her favourite place; a small landing that boasted a huge, brightly-coloured window. It rose up from the floor to the ceiling and on sunny days scattered rainbows of light on the walls. Today though, something had changed and the lights on the stairs began to flicker nervously. She sat, rooted to the spot, having had the undeniable sense that someone had just brushed past her.

Amelie!

A loud clap of thunder rattled the window panes and Amelie spun round. She scrambled to her feet and found herself gazing into the eyes of a very tall stranger. He stared down at her, mutely. With his long white hair and eyes like giant almonds he was the sort of man who would get more than a passing glance; and cause people to stare rudely and bump into lamp posts. 'Are you the roof man?' she whispered hoarsely.

Don't be silly, she told herself at once, trying hard to be brave though without much success. How could he possibly be, dressed like that – in a funny silver-coloured suit with a badge on his chest; like two hands clasping a globe...? Thoughts raced ahead of her and she froze, aware that this enormous stranger might actually do her harm. Even if she screamed, it was unlikely anyone would hear: with Mum busy in the studio, Tim lost in his trains, and well, Storm who was not only deaf, but also spent most of his time asleep. Her heart thundered in her ears.

Then something extraordinary happened. He reached out a long-fingered hand and wrapped an invisible blanket around her; it was warm and comforting and calmed her nerves a little. He spoke gently, his voice deep and sonorous:

'Amelie, your home is in great danger and, I'm afraid,

only you can save it…'

He knew about their house!

'You are our last hope.' With this he produced out of nowhere a tiny crystal. It shimmered with gold and flashes of blue. 'This precious Stone will protect you. Keep it on you at all times but tell no one about it. *No one!* Not yet.' Thereupon he placed it in her palm, bowed deeply then floated slowly upwards and finally disappeared out through the brightly-coloured window.

Amelie's hand flew to her mouth. She sat down again for a moment, examining the little crystal, turning it over in her hands. It was exquisite, so like the one Storm had sometimes told them about in his *Strange but True* stories. She tucked it safely away and, dazed with excitement, crept slowly downstairs.

'Quite enough hidden worlds for one day, I think,' she cautioned herself, padding along the hallway to the sitting room. She could already hear Tim talking to himself and the occasional snore from Grandpa Storm. Her hand rested a moment on the shiny brass door knob then, taking a deep gulp of air, she marched in, and closed the door firmly behind her.

Storm was dozing by the fire, wrapped in a tartan blanket, with Lara their Golden Retriever and Freddie the cat asleep at his feet. He was technically Great-Grandpa Storm, since their father and grandparents had all disappeared when they were both far too young to remember; killed in some tragic accident that no one ever spoke of anymore.

'Tim…' Amelie perched on a chair near the fire and tried to catch his eye. The old *Hornby Dublo Book of Trains* lay open on the table while he ferreted about in a carved wooden chest behind the sofa. Humming to himself, he hauled out a battered tin and a large cardboard box and tipped their contents on the floor. Lara, sensing a game, shook herself awake and came to inspect. Freddie, meanwhile, opened one eye. He yawned, stretched lazily and leapt onto Amelie's lap.

Amelie edged a little closer to the fire and toasted her toes. Somehow, the smell and crackle of burning logs made it seem much more like Christmas than mid-July. She waited, drumming her fingers on the arm of her chair. 'Tim, I've just seen a ten foot tall man on the stairs.'

Tim was now counting rail tracks, ready to assemble them. 'One, three, five, seven, nine – hey, there's a piece missing…' He searched around and eventually spotted it under Lara's tail. 'Stop being a weirdo,' he said, without looking up. Sisters could be so annoying at times.

Amelie crossed her arms in a sulk. 'I'm telling you, he was huge…'

On the floor lay a jumble of miniature locomotives, and platforms, some little figures too: a portly station master with a flag and a tiny whistle that actually worked. There were passengers with suitcases and umbrellas. All things their father and a generation of Trotts before him had enjoyed enormously.

'He also said our house is in great danger…'

Tim clipped together the tracks to form a large oval then added some platforms, a ticket office, and a signal box; and finally a handful of passengers and station employees. It was all beginning to take shape quite nicely. Suddenly, he stopped what he was doing and sniffed the air. 'Come to think of it, it probably is. Can't you smell that?'

'The oven!' Amelie picked up Freddie and dropped him on Tim's carefully planned railway, scattering platforms and station employees and passengers with their suitcases and umbrellas. She raced into the kitchen just as the smoke alarm went off.

'Cheers, Amelie!' Tim muttered, patiently restoring order to Havenbridge Junction.

Storm's nose twitched and, stirred from sleep, he sat bolt

upright. 'Fire!' he boomed, and promptly fell asleep again. Storm had a thing about fire.

'It's totally ruined!' Amelie returned, bearing the charred remains of the cake. 'Isla's coming and I'll be in terrible trouble again with Mum, and she hasn't even seen my report but then she'll see your brilliant one, and ...oh, we'll be homeless, and everything's going horribly wrong...' She took a gulp of air and began to run about in circles, stamping her feet as though performing some curious dance.

Tim bit his lip to stop himself laughing and wondered if she knew just how stupid she looked. 'I won't mention reports unless Mum asks. Anyway, she's too preoccupied with the house at the moment.'

Amelie stamped her foot again. '*Precisely*, our house is in danger and only I can...'

'Only you can what?' said Tim.

'Nothing.' Amelie's mind was elsewhere. Instinctively, she felt for the little crystal inside her pocket and was instantly rewarded with an idea. Charlie! She raced into the hallway, grabbed her waterproof, and returned at once with her purse.

'Where are you off to now?' Tim said, staring out at the rain. 'It's tipping down still.'

'Charlie's Bakery.' She began to count out the remains of her pocket money. 'I'll have to hurry though. He shuts at five and Isla's arriving at six. Come on Freddie, let's find your harness.'

'Put this to it then.' Tim fished out a shiny two pound coin from his pocket, his way of making amends for being unkind. Sometimes he forgot she was only ten.

'Burnt cake?' Storm bellowed and fumbled around in his old tweed jacket. He pulled out a crumpled note. It was funny how some days he was deaf as a white cat while other times could hear perfectly well. 'Here, get two then, and fetch me a Havenbridge Gazette while you're at it. Blasted

29

paper boy forgot it this morning.'

'Wow Storm, a fiver; thank you!' Amelie stuffed it inside her glove. 'By the way, I'm writing a book about you, and I've just seen a ten foot tall man on the stairs.'

The old man sank down in his chair and slowly adjusted his hearing aid, unsure if he had heard her correctly. 'Book about me? Ten foot tall man? Oh, my Lord...' He shook his head solemnly. 'So, he's back at last, is he?'

But Amelie and Freddie had already gone, leaving Tim somewhat nonplussed. 'What do you mean, *he's back*? Who's back?'

'The Commander,' Storm said grimly and shook his head. 'All I know is this, Tim. He only ever appears in times of trouble.'

Chapter Five
The End of the World

Tim wandered into the hallway and paused as a loud crash resounded in the attic. 'Is that you, Eggy?' he murmured, pulling on his jacket. 'What exactly are you trying to say?'

Aunt Eggy, short for Eglantyne, had been dead for over twenty years but, according to Storm, had taken up permanent residence in the attic. She roamed the house with a big stick, *tap-tap-tapping*, and ready to deal with intruders and children who didn't behave. Tim and Amelie were never quite sure whether they believed him, of course; but a bit of them did, even though they knew draughty old houses often made strange noises with clanking pipes and creaking floor boards, and things falling off shelves. Or the occasional door that slammed shut of its own accord.

Another crash from the attic; it seemed like their old house really was falling to bits.

'Amelie, wait!' Tim ran into the garden but she and Freddie had already disappeared from view. He gazed about him. Their beloved playhouse was flooded; such had been the volume of water unleashed from the skies. Two more bicycles lay abandoned, his own and Isla's, caught in a storm and left where they had been dismounted. He picked them up now and propped them against the garden wall before wandering back inside.

Amelie freewheeled down the hill to the church, past the little stone cottage where Isla lived and along Primrose Lane to a small row of shops on the outskirts of town. Seagulls wheeled overhead as she neared the coast. The worst of the storm had passed now but fields were waterlogged for miles around and the beaches deserted. Freddie who, unlike most cats, didn't mind a bit of rain, sat up in the wicker basket enjoying the ride.

At the bakery, Charlie had already cleared his window display but seeing Amelie he smiled and said he'd likely find something nice for her out the back. He returned, balancing a large cake on one hand, like a waiter.

'Good to see you again, m'dear, and Master Freddie too. Here you go then, one coffee and walnut and a chocolate sponge on its way.'

The storm had passed in more ways than one and Amelie breathed a sigh of relief. There might be just enough room in her basket if Freddie sat on top. However, when she emptied her glove onto the counter, she realised she hadn't quite enough money for two after all since she had to keep a pound back for Storm's Gazette.

Charlie shook his head and pretended to take them both away. Then he laughed and agreed to let her off the extra seventy pence, claiming she'd be saving his waistline as he'd only have scoffed them both for supper. He patted his enormous belly.

'Thank you, Charlie…' Amelie eyed him surreptitiously; he must have eaten an awful lot of cake to get that big. A hazard of the job, she supposed.

Charlie rang the money in the till. 'Having a bit of a do then, Amelie?'

'Kind of - my second-best friend Isla's coming to tea…' She pulled a face and groaned, '…and our cousin, Magnus too.'

'No way! Not that wretch, Bottomley-Sligh? Well, blow

me down, he's never related to you!'

''Fraid so, Charlie.'

'Him and his mates are banned from this shop. And half the others in Havenbridge, shouldn't wonder,' Charlie tutted. 'Rough lot; coming in here, smoking, and swearing at the missus! Wouldn't think he went to that posh school. I blame the parents.' He placed the cakes delicately inside two large cake boxes which he then wrapped in brown paper and tied with string. 'You know, one of them nicked our charity box while I was out the back. I swear it was him.'

'Magnus? Wow, that's terrible, Charlie. He's got loads of money too.'

'Said he'd have our place shut down for food poisoning if I dared report him; reckoned his dad's got contacts on the council.'

'Uncle Maynard? Oh, take no notice, Charlie. Magnus is all talk. He's always boasting his dad will knock our house down and build horrible new houses in its place.' Then a worried look passed over her face. Perhaps the Bottomley-Slighs were a bigger threat than they'd realised. 'Does that mean he can't eat any cake?'

'Too right! I'll give him food poisoning, 'orrible, smelly little fart, excuse my French…'

'I didn't realise you spoke French, Charlie. Anyway,' she said, remembering a few useful phrases Storm had once taught her, '*merci beaucoup* for the lovely *gateaux* and *au revoir*. I'd better get off for now.'

Charlie looked somewhat baffled. 'Call in anytime, my lovely. And remember me to old Storm.'

'Bye, Charlie, will do.'

'Hang on - have you heard today's news?'

Amelie shook her head. 'Only the weather forecast, I'm afraid. The Weather Man says *we've got deepening lows and vigorous depressions* on the way, which just means more rain, I think. By the way, I'm writing a book.'

'Book, eh?' Charlie smiled and said he would get her autograph and buy a copy for his wife once it was published. In fact, Charlie was so nice that Amelie was rather tempted to tell him about the ten foot tall man, but then something stopped her. He might think she was a bit funny in the head; or that an impossibly tall man like that was just a *figment of her imagination*, an annoying phrase used by grown-ups about most of Amelie's observations. This time, however, she had absolute proof, right here in her pocket, even though it had to remain a secret for now.

'I'll pick up Storm's newspaper on the way home. Thanks for reminding me, Charlie.'

'Yes, it's all in there.' Charlie lowered his voice. 'Strange lights over Havenbridge, down by the harbour, and up on Cloud Hill, near you. One of them followed the vicar home on his bike. And another chased Sergeant Buggeley in his police car – scared him half to death, though he'd never admit it.'

'Oh, dear,' Amelie said. 'That doesn't sound too good.'

'It's a sign, the missus says…'

'Sign of what, Charlie?'

'End of the World…'

Amelie quivered. 'Oh, Charlie, not more bad news please; it's the start of our holidays and I haven't even begun my book.'

The rain had eased off to a light drizzle now. There was even a glimmer of sunlight on the far horizon. Amelie placed her two packages in the wicker basket with Freddie perched on top, and pushed her bicycle up the steepest part of the hill, turning round now and then to check they weren't being followed by any more strange lights. No lights but a faint rainbow had appeared against the dark clouds. Isla always said rainbows were a sign of hope. Or was it really true what Charlie's wife said about the End of the World? Would they all wake up tomorrow and find nothing there?

Chapter Six
More Bad News, I'm Afraid

She stopped off at Patel's Newsagent's where nice Mrs Patel greeted her with a friendly wobble of her head and gave her a free lollipop. Then, tucking the newspaper into her basket, she continued up the hill to Hadleigh House, her mission successfully completed.

A white van had appeared in the drive; parked on the gravel outside the front porch. It had huge extending ladders on its roof and *Elias Dankstone, Bespoke Roofing & Building Services* painted on the side. Suddenly, she sneezed. A man was leaning against the van, smoking a cigarette. He had curly black hair and a tattoo of a snake on his neck and he looked like he needed a shave.

Seeing her, he grinned, revealing two gold teeth. 'Hello, darlin', you the lady of the house?' He looked up at the roof and sniffed. 'Big place you've got here.' He flinched somewhat, spotting Freddie in Amelie's basket. 'More of a dog man myself…'

'Mmm…' She sneezed again. She could imagine exactly the kind of dog he had in mind; straining at the leash with teeth bared and jaws dripping from its latest kill. Then she remembered. She'd seen him up here once before; lurking around at the far end of the garden while she was calling Freddie in for his supper.

'I'll get Mum,' she said, wheeling her bicycle round to the back of the house with the Gazette under one arm. She lifted Freddie out of the basket, removed the two now rather battered packages and hurried into the house.

'Roof man's here, Mum!'

Lucy was busy in the garden studio, preparing her latest canvas. Amelie loved its pleasantly oily smell of paint and turpentine. Dozens of little tubes of colours littered the surfaces with exotic names that sounded like they belonged to famous people: Scarlet Lake and Rose Madder. One painting there never failed to catch her eye. It dominated the whole studio: a life-size portrait of a man with shiny, dark hair and a very kind face.

'Michael...' Lucy would say with such a break in her voice that they didn't ask about him much anymore since her eyes always shone with tears when they did. Amelie worried about her mother a lot. Did this picture kind of keep him alive, she wondered? The face looked so real you half expected his mouth to open or his eyes to blink.

Looking up from her work, Lucy gave a little wave. 'Let Mr Dankstone in, will you, sweetheart? Tell him I'm on my way.'

'Do I have to? You know I'm a *lerjick*. He makes me sneeze.' Amelie set down her two packages, went through into the hallway and reluctantly opened the front door. Yes, it was definitely him all right, skulking about in the garden that night.

She left him in the hall then kicked off her trainers, hung up her waterproof and stole into the kitchen with the cakes. They were rather squashed now, thanks to Freddie, but she arranged them carefully on a couple of pretty china dishes, and carried them into the pantry for later. It was cold as a fridge inside but she loved to linger there all the same, savouring the delicious scent of herbs and spices from the little jars that lined the shelves. At one end of the pantry was an old broken-down servants' lift where banqueting dishes had once been transported to the upper floors. She imagined housemaids in black dresses and footmen in livery, carrying silver trays laden with the most mouth-watering fare. It was all making her feel quite hungry.

Amelie unscrewed one of the jars and scattered a handful of hundreds and thousands over the cakes. She eyed them hungrily. Thanks to Freddie's weight, buttercream had oozed out at the edges. No one would notice surely, would they? She ran a finger round each one, just to tidy them up a little then stood back to admire her work with a satisfied grin.

Meanwhile her mother and the Dankstone man were in the hallway, chatting about the state of the house. He was kicking skirting boards and pipes, patting walls and inspecting damp patches. It was a strange ritual with a lot of tut-tutting and shaking of his head. Then he put an arm round her mother's shoulders and promised her he'd put everything right. Amelie shuddered. She listened for a while then got bored and went into the sitting room to tell Tim and Storm the latest news.

'Charlie sent his regards and let me off the full price so I got two big ones but Magnus isn't allowed any as he's like totally forbidden to enter the shop ever again and that's for coming in with some rough kids and being rude to Charlie's wife and swearing and smoking and threatening Charlie, oh, and stealing a charity box off the counter. And I was like *Oh, Charlie, that's terrible...* Here...' She passed Storm his newspaper. 'Charlie says there's definitely something funny going on; lights chasing the vicar on his bike and scaring Sergeant Buggeley half to death. It's all about the End of the World.'

The old man opened his newspaper and grunted. 'Not surprising really with all the trouble in the world and weapons in the hands of lunatics... We'll all be blown up at this rate.' He picked up his magnifying glass to study the small print.

Amelie listened in horror. So, not only would they be homeless, they were now about to be blown up by lunatics too.

'Amelie…' Tim was about to mention the Commander when they heard the front door close and the white van set off down the gravel drive.

'It was him all right,' Amelie began, 'creeping around our garden that night.' Then their mother arrived and stared at all the mess on the floor. 'I guess you'd better clear that lot up, Tim,' she said, 'and Amelie, do something with that hair, it's a mess…'

Amelie shrugged. 'It's always a mess. Maybe I'll put it in bunches. Not that I'm making any effort for Magnus!'

Hearing this, Storm looked up from his paper. 'Leave the poor girl alone, Lucy. It's not what you look like, it's what's inside that matters. Anyway, she's beautiful just as she is. Like Eggy…'

'Thanks, Storm!' Amelie beamed.

'You're right, of course,' said Lucy, chastened. 'I'm just a bit stressed.'

Tim grunted. 'What about us? Think of our stress - two whole hours of Magnus; what a great start to the holidays this is. By the way, Mum, Magnus was caught stealing.'

'He's certainly a difficult boy,' Lucy agreed, remembering that time money had gone missing from her purse.

'Difficult?' Storm exploded. 'He's a flaming delinquent, Lucy!'

'I know, Storm, but my sister's got a party on tonight.'

'Half-sister,' Amelie corrected. 'You're nothing like her, Mum.'

'Ugh!' Tim looked like he'd swallowed a handful of worms. 'Will we even *recognise* her?' Mona's face, an unpleasant shade of sun-bed orange, had been reorganised so many times (new nose, cheek implants and an eye lift that gave her a look of permanent surprise) that no one could quite remember how she'd looked before.

'What has the world come to?' Storm muttered. He often asked this question though no one ever seemed to know the answer.

Lucy grinned. 'She's always been a bit on the flamboyant side.'

'She's always been jealous you married our Dad,' Tim said.

'And ended up...' Amelie made a sweeping gesture with her hand, '...with all this!'

'Well, she certainly won't be now then. She detests old houses. Anyway, she's redeemed herself a little today...'

'With Elias Dankstone, you mean?' Amelie scoffed.

'Come here and sit down, my dear, and tell me all about it,' said Storm kindly. 'You're looking very tired.'

'Not good news, I'm afraid, Storm.' Lucy squatted on the arm of his chair. 'The roof is about to collapse.'

'That's it then,' Amelie said, 'I'm definitely living outside! Even a doorway's better than this. I shan't sleep a wink tonight.'

'Don't worry, sweetheart. He'll be back tomorrow to sort it all out.'

'I'm scared it's a sign, the End of the World...'

'Don't be so silly, Amelie.'

'I mean it. Everyone says so, well, Charlie's wife anyway. And Storm says we'll be blown up by lunatics and Isla knows all about aliens coming and abducting people. I don't want to live on Mars. I like it here. And as for that awful man, I've seen him up here before... He makes me a *lerjick*...'

'Stop it, Amelie! What's this allergic nonsense anyway?'

'She's right, Mum,' said Tim. Storm's words had troubled him. Who exactly was this Commander and why had he come? 'It does feel like the end of the world, *our* world, at least. Seriously, you won't sell to Maynard, will you? He's had his eye on Hadleigh for years…'

'Whatever made you say that, Tim?'

'You've heard Mona – always going on about old houses and why we should have one of Maynard's hideous new ones, with plastic doors and a tiny square of grass for a garden, down on the Eastbridge Estate. I'd rather live in a tent!'

'And Magnus, boasting they'll knock our house down.' Amelie sat glumly, cradling her knees.

'Sell Hadleigh?' Storm thumped his walking stick hard on the floor, causing Freddie and Lara to scatter. 'Not on your Nelly! And certainly not to that crook, Bottomley-Sligh…'

'There's still so much that needs doing. Roof, damp course, rewiring, new boiler…'

'Hmm,' Storm grunted.

'Hmm,' echoed Amelie. 'Mr Dankstone sounds like an expert on everything though he doesn't look like he knows anything much at all.'

'Oh, Amelie,' Lucy laughed. 'We're actually lucky to have found him. Look, why not ask Isla to stay over tonight? She can have the nice guest room next to you.'

Amelie's spirits lifted a little. 'Really, Mum? Cool, I'll call her now, and I'm sorry about the cake. I got a bit interrupted but then thought of Charlie and we all clubbed together so it's all turned out right in the end!'

'Yes, very resourceful of you, my dear. But before you go…' Lucy reached out to tidy her hair. 'There, that's a bit better. I've put it in two nice plaits. Just needs a couple of hair bands now to keep them both in place. And, before I forget, where's your report?'

'In the post, I expect.' Amelie flushed deeply and hurried off to phone Isla. She would have to be even more *resorsfull* to wriggle out of that. There was always so much to worry about these days, especially now with the house and the End of the World. Sighing heavily, she promised she'd begin writing her book that night; tucked up in bed with a mug of hot chocolate.

I'll text Isla too, Tim decided, secretly pleased she was staying over too. She was quite good fun for a girl, though he would never actually say so. Clever and quick limbed, she was better at football than anyone he knew, even including himself; and she never minded getting mud on her clothes either.

He collected up the rails and locomotives and placed them all neatly inside the old wooden chest. Here too were all Storm's war medals and some rather faded hand-made Christmas decorations that dated back to the mid-1890s when Hadleigh House was first built. Just as he was about to close the lid he spied a small tin, right at the bottom, labelled *World War Two Aircraft and Airmen*. It was one he hadn't noticed before but would definitely take a proper look next time.

For now there were more urgent things to consider; above all, Storm's warning: *The Commander only ever appears in times of trouble*. He resolved to tell Amelie whenever they were next on their own. Right now he must figure out how best to deal with Magnus.

Chapter Seven

Isla Batty Comes to Stay

'I feel like I've known Isla forever,' Amelie confided to Storm as they waited for her to arrive. 'We only met her last month but I can't think of anyone I'd rather spend time with. Apart from well, like you and Mum and Freddie and Lara; and Tim, I suppose,' she added grudgingly since Tim hadn't believed her about the ten foot tall man.

'Then I'm sure you have,' the old man replied sagely, patting her hand. 'That kind of friendship is one to treasure.'

'Would you mind too much if she was my first best friend now? You're my only two friends in the world, apart from Tim but brothers don't count. I'll still love you exactly the same…'

Storm looked like a small boy about to have a tantrum. 'I would mind very much!' he roared, and then broke into peals of laughter. 'But of course not, my dear!'

'Oh, good, I'm glad you'll meet her at last. And I'm sure you'll love her as much as we do.'

'Yes, I'm certain I will.'

They had come upon Isla one fine afternoon before the rainstorms began. Tim and Amelie had wandered down to the sea, as they often did when the weather was good and there was little else to do. Visitors to Havenbridge always said how lucky they were to live by the sea. 'It must be like being on holiday all year round.' And it was. They couldn't ever imagine having to live somewhere else.

They arrived at a quiet little cove that they'd come to think of as their own, so it was quite a surprise to see a girl there already, skimming stones and looking out to sea. She appeared to be lost in thought, unaware of their presence. Spotting a likely new friend, Lara ran up to introduce herself.

The girl bent down and ruffled her coat. 'Hey, what a beautiful boy you are!'

Lara didn't seem in the least put out by this case of mistaken identity and licked her hand amiably. Suddenly, the girl let out a squeal of delight. Not wishing to be overlooked, Freddie had tagged along too and began to nuzzle her leg.

'Wow, a cat on a beach!' The girl glanced up and saw Amelie at the other end of Freddie's lead.

Amelie smiled. 'Freddie thinks he's a dog. He was abandoned as a kitten and Lara raised him.' She stooped to tickle his chin. 'You've already made friends with Lara then.'

The girl realised her mistake at once and laughed, flashing perfect white teeth. 'I'm sorry, Lara, what a pretty *girl* you are!'

She had curly black hair and gleaming, conker-brown skin; polished to a shine, like Storm's shoes. Her voice was intriguing, like someone in a film.

She offered Amelie her outstretched hand. 'My name's Isla, by the way: Isla Jane Batty. What about you?'

'Amelie Trott,' Amelie replied, cautiously avoiding her middle name. It was bad enough having wild carroty hair and no dad, and living in a house that was falling to bits; without having to admit to a name that was normally reserved for aunties and grannies. 'Come and meet my brother, Tim.' She gestured towards the sand dunes where Tim was securing their towels with stones. The two girls strolled along the beach to join him.

'I saw you skimming stones earlier,' Tim said, straightening up. 'Not bad for a girl.' He grinned. 'Did you know the ideal angle for skimming is twenty degrees?'

'But of course!' Isla knew she was good; her father had taught her and he was the best skimmer in the world.

Isla was half Afro-American – the Mom half, she explained. She was staying for the summer with her father, Dr Andrew Batty, and his sister, Georgina.

'In a little stone cottage at the bottom of Cloud Hill. Auntie George keeps an eye on me while Dad's at work at the hospital.'

'Cloud Cottage?' Tim raised his eyebrows. Funny they'd never seen her before. 'We're almost neighbours then. We live quite close, top of the hill.'

'I'm only here for the school vacation.' There was a look of sadness in her eyes. 'My dad works such long hours I don't get to see him much. It sucks!'

'You mean holidays? Well, you'll have ages here then,' Amelie said cheerfully. 'School doesn't start back till September.'

Isla shook her head. 'It's different across the pond.'

Amelie looked puzzled. 'Pond?'

'Atlantic Ocean,' she explained. 'In Washington we finish school early June which means I have to fly back to the States in August.'

'So soon?' Amelie felt a sudden wave of disappointment break over her. She had only just met Isla but it seemed like they were already good friends. 'We'll still be at school till mid-July but you can hang out with me and Tim at weekends if you like.'

'Yeah, not that anything much happens in Havenbridge. Not like Washington,' Tim said.

Isla's face brightened. 'It's my twelfth birthday next Saturday. Would you like to come? Mom's flying over so

44

you'll be able to meet her, and Dad's promised to take time off for my party.'

Isla's parents had split up when she was six. They used to live in London but soon after the divorce she and her American 'mom' Bettina moved to Washington where she now had a very important post at the British Embassy.

'Yes, please!' Amelie was ecstatic. A proper friend at last; already she was planning what she might give her for her birthday. 'We'll go, won't we, Tim?'

In the end, the whole family was invited to Isla's party: Mum, Storm, and Lara and Freddie too, though Freddie's invitation was apologetically withdrawn when Isla remembered Auntie George's cat hair allergy, and Storm had to decline because he needed his afternoon nap. Tim and Amelie made many more visits to Cloud Cottage though Isla had never come to Hadleigh House, till today.

'She's here!' Amelie watched on tiptoes as Dr Batty's car swung into the drive and came to a halt outside the kitchen window. She rushed outside with arms wide open to greet her. 'You're here at last – welcome to Hadleigh House!' She turned to wave to Dr Batty but he had already sped off to an emergency at Littlehaven Hospital.

'Here,' Tim said. 'Give us your bag and I'll show you your room.' He hitched Isla's overnight bag over one shoulder.

'Wait till you see!' Amelie cried, tugging at Isla's sleeve. 'We'll take you for a tour of the house; show you the Ballroom, and the attic where dead Aunt Eggy lives, just a peep as the ceiling's falling through, and then there's Mum's garden studio, and our playhouse, and tomorrow we'll ask Storm to show you his microlight plane in the hangar, and by the way…' She leaned to whisper something confidential in Isla's ear…

'Really?' Isla's eyes widened and she laughed. Her teeth were astonishingly white and her big smile, as always, took everyone by surprise. 'Awesome! How tall did you say?'

'Ten feet, at least - oh, and I'm writing a book, about Storm.' Should she tell her about Dorin too, she wondered? One day perhaps...

Isla grinned. Amelie was such fun to be around. And what a house! With an actual ballroom and a ghost in the attic; plus an airplane in the garden... too much! 'That sounds amazing, guys. Amelie, I love your braids, by the way!'

'Plaits, you mean?' Amelie said. 'Mum did them but I prefer bunches...'

'We'll have a game of football later if it clears up,' Tim added, just to annoy his sister.

Amelie pulled a face. 'Magnus won't want to play.'

'Magnus?'

'Don't worry, Isla,' said Amelie. 'He's only here for a couple of hours. We can easily ignore him.'

Just then, Lucy appeared in the doorway, wiping her hands on her smock. 'Poor Isla, why don't you come in out of the cold?'

'Thanks so much for inviting me, Mrs Trott. Here, these are for you,' Isla said, producing a very large box of hand-made chocolates, gift-wrapped with a big red bow. 'Just for you, Dad says, and not to be shared!'

Lucy's face broke into a broad smile. What a breath of fresh air Isla was. 'How kind! Thank you, Isla, and do call me Lucy, or Auntie, if you'd rather,' she added, just grateful Amelie had a proper friend at last. 'Mrs Trott makes me sound so old.'

'Now you're definitely part of the family!' Amelie beamed, linking Isla's arm.

'Awesome!' Isla laughed.

'Arsum!' Amelie mimicked. It was so cool to say American things like jelly instead of jam, or cookies for biscuits.

'Alright then,' Isla said, 'Aunt Lucy it is.'

Aunt Lucy then went on to apologise for the state of the house, which she always did when someone new came though no one ever did mind really. Most people thought it was an *interestingly messy house* with lots of unusual things to look at and admire.

'We'll eat in here tonight, I think. Save carrying it all through to the dining room.' The truth was the dining room table was already piled high with unpaid bills and unanswered letters; and unfinished sketches and tubes of oil paints that had somehow found their way from the garden studio into the house. 'Meanwhile, why don't you two show Isla around before Magnus arrives?'

They trouped off with Tim in the lead, leaving Lucy to seek out Aunt Eggy's antique dinner plates. 'Wait,' she called after them, having carefully placed them on the dresser ready for their meal, 'do give Storm a shout too, on the way…'

Chapter Eight
A Tour of Hadleigh House

'Ladies and gentlemen...' Tim harrumphed, and adopted a rather plummy tour guide's voice. 'Hurry along now, please,' he called to an invisible gathering of visitors and the two girls giggled.

'Home to the Trott family for generations, Hadleigh was once renowned for its weekend parties and masquerade balls.' He peered at them over imaginary spectacles. 'Here, according to legend, are hidden passages filled with treasure; and a magical Stone that promises good fortune for its keeper...'

He gestured towards a heavy oak door with a shiny brass handle, then flung it open and shepherded them into the room. Lara came bounding to greet them. 'And here, ladies and gentlemen, we have the elegant sitting room.'

'Ah, bless! See how pleased she is to see you again!' Amelie said, patting Lara's coat.

'And my cute little friend Freddie,' Isla cried. 'I'll swear he just spoke!'

Freddie took a moment to sniff her outstretched hand then reasonably satisfied, curled his tail round her legs and chirruped. He was the friendliest little cat she had ever seen.

'Right, Storm, you can wake up now!' Amelie shook the old man's arm gently. 'This is Isla.'

'Eileen?' He opened one eye and stroked his moustache thoughtfully.

'No, Isla. Like island without the 'nd',' Tim said patiently, as though he were talking to a small child.

'Ireland?' he barked. 'What kind of blasted name is that?'

'I-S-L-A, Storm... Oh, never mind.' Amelie took Isla's hand and pulled her towards the door. 'Let's see the rest of the house.'

Storm chuckled to himself, having heard her perfectly well the first time.

But Isla was enchanted and paused to take in the room. It was a bit shabby and cobwebby but beautiful all the same. She had never seen such a place before. Like a museum with so many old and interesting things: shelves of stuffed birds and animals in glass cases (beloved pets of past generations, she wondered?), porcelain dolls with real hair, and oriental rugs and wall hangings.

'And Mum says to give you a shout, Storm,' Tim said, shooing the girls into the tiled hallway. 'Magnus is coming.'

The old man grunted.

'Wow, look at these – how cool is that!' Isla stopped to admire two uncannily life-like portraits of Amelie and Tim. 'Your mom is so gifted. These are more real than a photograph!' There was also a small sketch of Storm, looking very dapper in his blue checked shirt and shiny brown shoes. 'Storm, super-cool name! He's a bit scary though, isn't he? I can see why you call him that.'

'He's just a big softy really,' Amelie laughed. 'You'll soon get to know him.'

'You'll see Mum's studio later,' Tim promised. 'Let's go upstairs now.'

They stopped on the landing by the stained glass window. 'I've been longing to show you this,' Amelie whispered. 'It's where I saw him, the ten foot tall man. He said I had to save our house.' It felt like the crystal was about to burn a hole in her pocket. If only she could show them both. 'Tim doesn't believe me though.'

'Oh, but I do,' Isla replied. 'It's quite magical here…'

Tim had the grace to look sheepish. 'Actually, I do, Amelie. Storm even knows who he is…'

'You mean you told him…?'

'Of course, but you'd already left. Apparently he's called the Commander and always turns up in times of trouble.'

'See, I told you it's the End of the World.'

Tim frowned. 'It does sound a bit ominous, I know.'

Isla shot him a startled look. 'You mean something bad is about to happen?'

Tim pursed his lips thoughtfully. 'In a way it already has: *Magnus*! We definitely can't talk about this with him here.'

'Well, this makes Washington extremely boring in comparison… And you said nothing ever happens in Havenbridge!' She gazed around her. What a fascinating old house this was; a bit shadowy and creepy in places but beautiful all the same. 'When was it built, Tim?'

'1895 - by Storm's grandfather, Theodore Sebastian Trott.' Tim quite liked to flaunt his good memory for dates. 'There's a plaque at the front of the house.'

'I like that big window best, especially the figure, surrounded by moons and stars; it's beautiful, like a cathedral.'

'That was added much later, Aunt Eggy's idea.'

Footsteps echoed from the floor above them and Isla laughed. 'She likes to let you know she's still around!'

They climbed another flight of stairs to the Ballroom where long ago the Trott family held their glamorous parties and balls.

It was the largest room in the house and took up much of the first floor. Faded wallpaper had long since begun to peel, exposing layers of colour beneath it; huge windows were draped with old velvet, and dusty chandeliers hung from the ceiling, laced with cobwebs. At one end of the room was a rickety table tennis table with a broken net and at the other end a little stage.

Isla jumped up with an imaginary microphone and began to sing. There was an old wind-up gramophone there too with records in brown paper sleeves. 'Let's have a party!' she laughed, grabbing Amelie's hand. 'You should definitely use this again. Parties, like, every weekend.'

'One day perhaps,' Amelie said wistfully and at once the Ballroom door swung shut behind them. 'I think Eggy likes that idea too!'

'Look at this!' Isla was spellbound. 'I just love old things...' She peered into a huge walk-in wardrobe, crammed with moth-eaten clothes and an assortment of shoes that spilled out of a tatty old cardboard box.

'Grandma Joan's,' said Amelie, giving Tim a strange look. 'She died in an accident, along with our dad and Grandpa Ted the year I was born. Since "That Terrible Day" as we call it, Mum can't bear to throw anything out.'

'Whoa! How awful to lose all your family like that,' Isla said, wondering if she might dare to ask more. 'Sorry, perhaps I shouldn't ask...'

Tim shrugged as though it was the most normal thing in the world to lose your dad and grandparents all in one day in an accident that no one ever spoke of anymore. 'No, it's fine really,' he answered in a very grown-up way. Just as Storm had when they last tried to bring the subject to light. 'It was a boating accident, we think. After having been missing for weeks, their bodies were washed up on the shore. Someone spotted them...'

'Kenny Pratt from the Fishing Tackle shop,' Amelie said. 'He ran off to sound the alarm...'

'But when the Emergency Services arrived, they'd all disappeared! Gone, no sign of them at all...'

'Disappeared, how come?'

'Nobody knows,' said Tim, 'though it was national news at the time. Storm says it finished poor Great-Grandma Louisa off. She died of a stroke soon after…'

'Poor, poor Grandpa Storm…'

They stood there looking at their feet until Amelie broke the silence: 'Maybe one day we'll know what really happened.'

'I'm sure you will,' Isla said and gave Amelie one of her beautiful smiles. Then she reached inside the wardrobe and fished out a couple of Edwardian handbags and a faded taffeta ball gown. 'I guess these must be Aunt Eggy's then …' She held the gown to her face and sank down into a little armchair that had lost most of its stuffing. 'I adore the smell of old things, don't you? Tell us more about Eggy then, Tim.'

Tim resumed his tour guide's voice:

'The Trotts share their house with the ghost of a madwoman called Eglantyne Trott who, word has it, restlessly paces the corridors and entertains *visitors from other worlds*. Hardly somewhere you'd wish to spend the night!'

Isla laughed and turned to Amelie. 'Hey, do you think you slipped randomly into another world earlier, Amelie?'

'Like another dimension, you mean? Maybe I did.' Amelie examined her wrist and began to wonder about Dorin. There was still a tiny red mark where he had grabbed her; and every bit as real as the little gold and blue crystal in her pocket.

Isla said she could almost see Aunt Eglantyne. If she half closed her eyes there she was, young and beautiful and dressed in her taffeta ball gown, dancing wildly to one of the records on the old wind-up gramophone.

'She was a very famous female explorer,' Amelie said, 'in the days when girls didn't do many exciting things.'

'Everyone thought she was mad,' Tim said. 'She wasn't, of course; just a bit eccentric, perhaps. She travelled all over the world: South America, India, Tibet, Nepal, and China…'

Isla nodded slowly. 'That'll account for all those unusual rugs and hangings in the sitting room.'

'Storm says we're kindred spirits,' Amelie said proudly. 'Let's do upstairs now though or we'll be late for tea.'

On the next floor was a spacious bathroom with black and white tiles and a colourful mural of seagulls on a deserted beach. Further along were two musty old bedrooms that nobody used anymore.

'This one's yours then, Isla,' Tim said with a totally straight face. He opened a door to reveal bare floorboards and a heap of suitcases and broken furniture. 'Despite their apparent good fortune, the Trotts have since fallen on hard times, and sadly the old house grows more ramshackle by the year…'

They continued along the corridor until they came to a large sign, affixed to one of the doors:

T. M. TROTT - NO UNAUTHORISED PERSONS BEYOND THIS POINT.

'My room,' Tim said as though no one could read.

Further along was Amelie's room. 'Ooh, how grand – 'Novel in Progress'!' said Isla. 'I'm so impressed.'

'Er, if you don't mind, we'll give mine a miss,' Amelie said, grabbing her hand. 'It's a bit of a mess…'

'Who cares about mess? You're a writer, Amelie! You don't have time to tidy rooms.'

Amelie gazed at her new friend in awe. Isla always managed to say exactly the right things.

'Okay, now your bedroom, Isla,' Tim said. 'Let's leave your stuff here.' The door was already open, revealing a freshly painted room with a bright rug and pretty chintz curtains and a little balcony overlooking the garden. He tossed Isla's bag on the bed.

'Hey, this is perfect!' Isla was spellbound. It had to be the nicest room she'd ever seen.

Feeling a sudden pang of hunger, Tim hurried them on to a steep flight of stairs. 'Last stop, the attic…'

'So, where does Storm sleep then?' Isla enquired. There were surely too many stairs for an old man to climb.

'Downstairs, next to his study…' Tim ran up the narrow steps ahead of them. 'And finally…' he opened the attic door just enough for Isla to peer in.

'Our dad was once a keen amateur astronomer. That's his telescope by the window. I can just remember someone lifting me up to look at the stars.'

'I guess that was him,' Isla remarked thoughtfully. She gasped suddenly, catching sight of a broken dolls' house. It sat on a mahogany table, alongside a handsome oak cupboard with a broken padlock.

'That once belonged to Storm's youngest sister, Maggie,' Amelie said. 'I loved that little doll's house when I was little.'

'So many beautiful treasures,' Isla observed, overlooking the buckets, half-filled with rainwater from the holes in the roof. 'I could stay here forever.'

Next to the attic were three little turret rooms, once used by the maids and housekeeper. Here, another narrow flight of stairs, the back stairs, took them down to the kitchen and basement scullery, and finally to the dining room where, through the French doors, they could see Lucy at work in her garden studio.

'It was once known as the morning room,' Tim informed Isla. 'Mum uses it because of the light.'

Isla watched, entranced. 'I'd love to be able to paint like your mom.'

'We'd better leave the basement for today,' Amelie said, 'it's only full of rubbish anyway.'

'And tunnels,' Tim joked. 'Not that we've ever found them. I wonder what's for tea…'

'I know!' Amelie skipped on ahead of them. 'It's my absolute favourite, Homity pie!'

They made their way back to the kitchen where the delicious smell of roasting onions and potatoes greeted them. The windows ran with condensation and Tim rubbed a patch clear with his sleeve. Outside it was still raining a little and the wind had got up, scattering twigs along the path. They all sat down at the old scrubbed table and waited for Lucy to join them.

Hearing their voices, Freddie and Lara wandered in. They eyed their empty bowls dolefully, hopeful for food.

'Now tell me about Magnus,' Isla said. 'What's he really like?'

Amelie scattered a handful of kibble in Lara's bowl. 'Gross. Like his dad. You won't like him either.'

'You haven't yet had the dubious pleasure of meeting Maynard, have you?' Tim said with a grin.

'Magnus once stole money from Mum...' Amelie said, emptying a tin of cat food into Freddie's dish and pulling a face. 'That smells disgusting, Freddie!'

'No way!'

'And Charlie's charity box too.'

'How sad,' Isla said. 'But even bad people can change. I guess we should still try to be nice to them even if they're not nice to us.'

'Yeah, well, good luck with that one,' said Tim wryly. 'Here's your chance now. I'm out of here.'

An enormous, black car had swept up the drive and with a squeal of brakes came to a halt by the kitchen door. 'Tell Mum I'm not feeling too well.' He coughed fairly convincingly and clutched at his chest. 'And mention I'll have my tea in bed.'

'Don't you dare,' Amelie said, 'you're not leaving me here alone with Magnus. Tim... Come back here now!' But Tim had already disappeared and she turned to Isla and sighed. 'I'd actually hate to be Magnus, you know. For one thing, you'd have to change your name, wouldn't you? Can you imagine – *Magnus Bottomley-Sligh?* Even Trott sounds fairly normal after that,' she added, feeling grateful for that one small gift of ordinariness. Strangely, for the first time in her life, she felt a tiny bit sorry for Magnus even though he'd done such terrible things. Perhaps it was the crystal. She reached into her pocket to check it was still there.

Or was it Isla? She always looked for the best in people. Magnus was rich, it was true, but what else did he have in his life? And despite everything and just for that moment, she wished Magnus could be as contented as she was when she was mind-wandering or spending time with her best friend Isla.

Chapter Nine

Magnus Bottomley-Sligh

But the feeling didn't last very long. 'I'm dreading this,' Amelie admitted, peering through the misted-up window. 'They're still talking, I think. No, hang on; Magnus is getting out of the car…' Then, hearing Tim's almost convincing cough, she spun around gladly. 'Thank goodness, you're back.'

Tim was wearing an old blue dressing gown over his clothes and a muffler wrapped round his throat. He had drawn bright red spots on his face and legs. 'I'm highly contagious,' he warned.

'Here…' Amelie held out her arm. 'Draw some on me…'

Isla laughed helplessly. 'You're crazy the pair of you! Won't your mom be mad?'

Tim grinned. 'Probably.' He straightened his face and opened the door. There, lolling against the wall was a pasty, thick set boy, busily engaged with his mobile phone. Magnus Bottomley-Sligh may have been only thirteen but this, Tim knew, was precisely how he would look in thirty years' time.

'Hi guys,' Magnus said cheerily, striding into the kitchen. 'Great to see you again!' He held up his hand to give Tim a high-five.

'We're all highly *contajius*,' Amelie said, rather taken

aback by the New Magnus. She glanced at Isla. Perhaps people really could change after all…

'Dengue fever,' Tim croaked, saying the first thing that came into his head. He'd heard Mrs Patel mention it once in the shop. 'You really don't want it.'

Magnus withdrew his hand and backed out of the door. 'Right, I'd better tell Mona…'

Mona Bottomley-Sligh was reapplying her lipstick. 'What's up, Nussy? Go back in and find those keys.'

'No way am I going back there,' he wailed. 'They're all covered in spots, I might die.'

His mother shuddered. 'Fleas from that ghastly cat, darling.' She drew a twenty pound note out of her wallet and waved it under his nose. 'Just put on a smile like I told you.'

'I did.' He snatched the money and twisted his mouth into something vaguely resembling a smile. 'And it's killing me.' Spending time with the Trotts was not his idea of a great night out.

'No, Nussy, a real smile, like this…' She grinned hideously. 'Easy once you think what we'll have in return.'

'I think you mean *me*,' Magnus said nastily. 'Hadleigh's all mine once you and Maynard croak. Unless he demolishes it first, of course…' It had never occurred to him to call his parents Mum and Dad like other children did. And as for him actually liking them…

Mona shrugged and began to rearrange her hair. 'Once we've access to those tunnels, you won't need the ghastly old house anyway. There's an absolute gold mine down there.'

'What about that Stone thingy though…? Maynard said the old psycho knew where it was.' His face changed suddenly. 'He's not still around, is he? You know how I hate his guts.'

'Storm? No,' his mother lied, vigorously shaking a can of

58

hairspray, 'he'll be in a home by now; or dead.'

'Six feet under!' Magnus laughed maliciously. 'Bleuh! What's that stink?'

Mona ignored him and patted her hair. 'You go back in and I'll follow. All we need is keys. Kitchen drawers are always a good bet. Or maybe try her bag like last time…'

Magnus scowled and heaved himself out of the car. 'This had better be worth it, Mona,' he growled, stuffing the money into his pocket.

'I nearly forgot this.' The New Magnus dumped a large overnight bag on the floor and reached out a pudgy hand to Isla. 'So you must be…?' He bared his teeth like an angry dog.

'Isla,' she replied.

'Cool,' said the New Magnus, looking her up and down and pretending to be impressed, 'great to meet you, Isla. Nice accent too.'

'I'm part American,' said Isla, wondering whether Amelie and Tim had exaggerated a bit. He didn't seem too bad really, apart from the angry dog face.

Mona entered in a suffocating cloud of scent. 'I'm a *lerjick*,' Amelie sniffed, willing her mother to come quickly and do something about the worrying overnight bag on the floor. 'Mum will be here soon. She's painting.'

'Painting?' Mona questioned with an air of self-importance. She flung herself down on the nearest chair. 'Some of us have real work to do… Ah, there you are, Lucy darling…'

'I'm so sorry, Mona,' Lucy said, breathlessly. 'I rather lost track of time. Tim, what on earth's up with your face?' She peered at him suspiciously. 'And your legs…'

'Fleas…' Mona said, recoiling.

'Dengue fever,' Tim insisted.

'Dengy what? Hmm,' Lucy said sharply. 'And Isla, is this yours, sweetheart?' She pointed to the mystery bag on the floor. 'Amelie, I thought you'd taken it up to her room.'

Amelie sighed theatrically. 'It's not Isla's.'

'You don't mind too much, do you, darling?' Mona simpered. 'Magnus so *loves* staying over - don't you, angel?'

The strange New Magnus nodded mutely, his face beginning to throb with so much smiling.

Lucy frowned. 'I don't know, Mona, with the state of the house and everything. There's nowhere...'

Thank you, Mum! Tim and Amelie chorused silently.

'Except maybe the study, next to Storm...'

Oh, why did you have to say that?

'Anyway, looks like our food's nearly ready,' Lucy said, inspecting the pie. 'So, wash your hands, everyone. And face and legs,' she said, looking at Tim. 'Ten minutes and we'll eat.'

Mona pulled back her sleeve to reveal an enormous gold watch. 'Oh, my days, is that really the time?' She pressed a sticky red kiss on Magnus's cheek and another twenty pound note in his hand.

'Liar,' he hissed and scrubbed at his face with his sleeve. 'You owe me double now. I thought he was dead.'

Mona's face darkened; from Cadmium Orange to Burnt Umber, observed Amelie, who knew every single colour on her mother's paint chart. How odd Mona looked with her thick black brows and stuck on eyelashes. Like Charlie who had once dressed up as an Ugly Sister in a production of *Cinderella* by the Havenbridge Players. And how ever did she walk on those enormous heels?

'I'll drop Magnus off after breakfast then, Mona,' called Lucy, halfway out of the door again, 'before Mr Dankstone starts on the roof.'

'Fabulous!' Mona gushed. 'We don't know him personally, of course, but I've heard he's amazing, very reasonable too...' But Lucy had already hurried off to warn Storm he had company that night. That probably wouldn't go down too well.

Mona rose, ready to plant another sticky red kiss on Magnus's cheek. This time, however, he swerved to avoid it, causing her to lose balance and career across the kitchen tiles, finally plummeting spread-eagled against the dresser. The force of her landing dislodged a pile of old china plates and sent them crashing to the floor.

Magnus's laughter was like shattering glass.

'Not Aunt Eggy's plates!' Amelie gasped loudly above the din. 'Mum will go mad.'

'Never mind plates, what about me!' Mona picked herself up and teetered across the tiles to the door.

'Hey, Magnus,' Isla said, practising the art of being nice to people, even though they might not be nice in return. 'Tell me about yourself. What would you like to be once you leave school?'

'Be?' He laughed as though this was the funniest thing he'd ever heard. What kind of stupid question was that? Then he remembered to be nice and gave her an oily smile.

'Oh,' Amelie cut in brightly, 'I'm going to be what I already am - an author.'

'You!' Magnus shouted, completely forgetting himself. 'But you're thick! I don't think so!'

'She's loads cleverer than you,' Tim growled, pretending to stamp on Magnus's foot.

Amelie blushed. Magnus hadn't changed one bit. If anything he'd got worse, worse even than her wretched Voice of Doubt.

Just then Storm appeared in the doorway. 'Even I heard that, you obnoxious lout!' he thundered. He sat down at the table and banged his fist so hard that everyone jumped.

Amelie tried to speak but the words still stuck in her throat. How could she ever have felt sorry for such a hateful boy? Tears stung her eyes till they shone like emeralds.

Isla squeezed her arm. 'Take no notice, girl,' she

whispered. 'You'll be a great writer one day, I just know it. And you know what? I'm going to be a pilot and have my own plane.'

'Quite right!' Storm patted Isla's hand. 'And good for you too, young woman; we had some damn good girls in the war. ATAs, we called them.' He turned to Tim and Amelie. 'My Louisa was one of them. Flew Tiger Moths, Spitfires; the lot. That's how we first met.'

'Great-Grandma? I didn't know girls could be pilots,' Tim said.

'But of course,' Isla said firmly. 'Girls can be absolutely anything they want: astronauts, scientists, engineers... boys too, of course. You just have to believe in yourself.'

Magnus rolled his eyes and pretended to yawn.

'Idiot,' Tim sighed.

'Idiot, eh?' Magnus squeaked. 'You're the idiots, the lot of you. You wait till I have this place...'

'Over my dead body!' Storm barked.

'Preferably,' Magnus sneered.

'Dead bodies?' Lucy enquired, arriving with two bottles of lemonade. 'I certainly hope not. Here, Isla, try some of this - Storm's speciality.' She filled Isla's glass. 'By the way,' she added, looking at Storm, 'I must be imagining things but I swear I saw someone on the stairs earlier... very tall.'

'Oh dear,' Storm said. 'That's twice today...'

Tim and Amelie exchanged glances.

'Anything I can do?' asked Magnus, quickly retrieving his smile. He had to act fast now and find those spare keys. 'More spoons for dishing up?' he said slyly, rifling through the kitchen drawers.

'No thanks, Magnus; it's all under control.' Lucy opened the oven door. The pie had a perfect golden crust, bubbling at the edges. 'It's your favourite, Amelie - Homity Pie.' She carried it to the table and wiped her brow with a sleeve. 'With roast potatoes, carrots and peas, all courtesy of Storm's vegetable garden. Now, where are those lovely old plates? I'm sure I left them here on the dresser.'

'In the bin,' Tim said bluntly.

'Oh, Amelie!'

'It wasn't me!' Amelie grumbled. 'Mona smashed them on her way out.'

'Stupid woman,' said Storm. 'Should wear proper shoes…'

'Unbelievable,' said Lucy, fuming, 'I got them out especially for Isla. Ah well, I suppose we'll just have to make do…'

#

'First class, as ever, Lucy, my dear…' Storm patted his mouth with a napkin. 'Do we get to sample those cakes now Amelie, or what?'

'On their way,' Tim shouted from the pantry, 'just sorting them out.' He turned to Amelie and whispered: 'Did you hear that earlier? Mum's seen the Commander too!'

'Sounds like it,' Amelie said, leaning against the old broken-down lift. 'By the way, thanks for sticking up for me like that. Magnus has completely ruined Isla's stay, hasn't he? She'll never want to come back, you know.'

Tim groaned. 'Yeah, and to think he's staying all night too…' He paused to inspect the cakes. 'Have you been at these already?'

Amelie blinked innocently.

'Finger marks in the buttercream?'

'Freddie sat on them so they needed a bit of tidying up. Is it true, Tim, about them buying our house?'

'The Slighs? How can they? It's not for sale.'

'Even so, we won't let them, will we? Not ever.'

'No, not ever.'

They carried the cakes aloft like trophies to the table.

'Thanks but I couldn't eat another thing, Auntie Lucy.'

Isla leaned back in her chair with a satisfied sigh.

'I could though,' said Magnus, his eyes devouring the remains of the cake. 'Any more going?'

'No, Magnus, we must save some for tomorrow,' Amelie said dismissively. 'Anyway, Mum - me and Tim will clear up tonight, won't we, Tim? Pass me an apron someone...'

Tim was about to protest since it wasn't his turn but then he caught on. One good way of avoiding Magnus, he supposed.

'Why don't you all help,' said Lucy, filling the kettle for coffee, 'then perhaps you can watch a film...?'

Chapter Ten

Storm and his Magical Stone of Power

'What's that dreadful racket?' growled Storm, as they gathered around the fire in the sitting room. 'Turn that rubbish down this minute!'

Magnus, who had no intention of cleaning anyone's kitchen, had fallen asleep on the sofa with a strange, discordant sound coming from his ears.

'Death Metal,' Tim said, seizing his ear phones. Magnus stirred and let out a loud snore.

Amelie squatted on the floor next to Storm's chair. 'Ignore him, let's play *Strange but True*. You go first, Storm. You'll love his stories, Isla. But please wait for me though...' She stood up suddenly. 'As I'm turning your stories into a book, Storm, I'll need to make some notes.'

Storm chuckled and said how honoured he was but doubted if anyone would really want to read it. Then seeing Amelie's face fall he swiftly changed his mind. 'Yes, of course, my dear, a certain best-seller!'

Isla sat cross-legged, gazing up at him. 'Yes, please, Mr Trott!' He was reading his newspaper with glasses *and* a magnifying glass. Imagine, only six years off a hundred; she'd never met anyone so old.

'The parachute one,' said Tim.

Magnus stirred. Oh no, he thought miserably, not more

of his boring back-in-the-day stories, please. I'll slope off in a bit to find those keys. And more cake.

'Good Lord,' Storm protested, 'you've heard that one a dozen times already.'

'Yes,' said Amelie, returning with her notebook and pen. 'The one with the magical Stone of Power.'

Magnus sat up suddenly. Did she really just say that?

Storm peered at him sternly over his glasses. 'Right then, unanimous.' He folded his newspaper, wrapped the tartan blanket around his legs, and began. 'This story is set during World War Two, in the winter of 1944 to be exact....'

'It was a clear, starlit night with a bright quarter moon. A young Flying Officer was returning home after a bombing raid on a munitions site in Germany when suddenly he spotted a strange looking aircraft alongside him. It appeared and disappeared, as though switching itself on and off. For a moment he wondered if he'd dreamed it; a mirage or something, brought on by tiredness. All he wanted now was to get back to base and have a nice cup of tea and a damned good sleep.

But sadly, a moment later a blast of cannon fire hit the starboard wing. The noise of the flames over the engine was intense. 'Right, my lad,' he told himself bravely but not without terror in his eyes. 'Chop! Chop!' There was only one thing for it…

Parachute at the ready, he leapt from the plane, only seconds before it exploded. But there were yet more dangers awaiting him. He would likely be spotted and, if not shot down, taken prisoner at least. However, something extraordinary was happening at the very same time. Two more strange aircraft appeared at incredible speed, creating an unexpected distraction for the enemy anti-aircraft crew on the ground.

His parachute billowed above him and he drifted down, silently, invisibly, and landed safely in a soft, grassy field.

The young flying officer watched as the strange aircraft continued their stunts, miraculously untouched by the enemy gunfire on the ground.

Then, looking down, he spied something glinting in the starlight; a small piece of glass in the grass. He reached out his hand and there it was, not glass at all as it turned out, but a beautifully formed piece of crystal.

He saw it as his lucky charm - every airman had one in those days, of course; a reminder that, despite danger, he was being looked after and was extremely fortunate to be alive. That little crystal stayed with him throughout the duration of the war.'

Storm wiped a tear from his eye and patted his trouser pocket. 'And it still remains close to him to this day. So, there you have it, Isla; a very strange story indeed but true, all the same.'

Isla was bewitched. The old man no longer scared her. She had been watching him throughout and noticed how radiant his face had become; no longer old but a much younger version of himself.

'So it was you all along, Mr Trott!'

'Yes, my dear, and as Tim and Amelie will tell you, that's why I still have a terrible aversion to fire.'

'There's more though, isn't there?' Tim prompted.

'Wait,' Amelie pleaded, furiously scribbling. 'I can't keep up!'

'Well,' said Storm more slowly, 'if all that wasn't all strange enough, my little crystal was exactly the same as a piece I'd once found in the attic. Part of my Aunt Eglantyne's collection and one I was especially drawn to as a child. Eggy insisted it must never leave this house.'

'Could we see it?' Isla asked.

'My magic Stone?' Storm shook his head and tapped his trouser pocket again. 'Call me superstitious but I prefer to keep it in here.'

Magnus smirked as an idea began to take form.

'Eggy had some very strange-but-true stories of her own,' the old man continued. 'The family thought she was mad and wanted her put away.'

'So where is her crystal now, Mr Trott?' Isla asked.

Storm lowered his voice. 'In my study, locked inside the roll-topped desk, where it can't fall into the wrong hands.'

So, there were *two*! Magnus was beside himself. He'd keep one and sell the other to Mona and Maynard.

Amelie looked up from her note-taking. How on earth would the Stone be safe with Magnus in the study? 'What happened to her stories then, Storm?' she asked. 'Did she write any of them down?'

Storm pinched her cheek fondly. 'Like you, Eglantyne was a very keen writer. And like me too, she detailed everything in a set of diaries: expeditions to the Far East and South America, encounters with strange persons, even information about the tunnels...'

Magnus did his best not to squeal.

'So what happened to them?' Tim asked.

'I suspect she hid them upstairs in the attic or Ballroom perhaps though they've never been found. Anyway,' he hinted obscurely, 'they'd be the key to many unsolved mysteries. If they're still around today, they could be extremely valuable.' He glanced at Magnus knowingly. 'Could even fetch millions, who knows?' He folded his blanket and started to gather up his things. 'But for now that little crystal is all that's left of her extraordinary life.'

Magnus swung his legs off the sofa. Yes, he would definitely find them! At this rate, he'd never have to do a day's work in his life.

'Hear that?' Tim tilted his head. There were the little footsteps again.

'She's heard us, discussing her diaries.' Amelie looked pointedly at Magnus. 'Don't anyone go near the attic.

There's no light up there for one thing and ghosts have a way of dealing with intruders.'

Magnus glanced at her scathingly. 'No such thing, you moron...'

'No ghosts?' bellowed Storm. 'Good Lord, you've a lot to learn, young man!' He heaved himself out of his chair. 'Now, if you'll all excuse me, I'm feeling rather tired.' He picked up his paper. 'I'll bid you all goodnight then and see you again in the morning.'

Chapter Eleven

A New Hope

'You now, Amelie,' Isla said. 'I heard what your mom said earlier. Tell us more about your ten foot tall man!'

Amelie shook her head. 'Not now.' She knew Magnus, and the Commander, as Storm called him, was far too special to be made fun of. 'Let's watch a film instead.'

'Er, no thanks...' Magnus sidled towards the door. 'I'd rather watch *Curse of the Dark Hearts* on my phone.' At least now, thanks to that idiot Storm, he knew exactly where to find those two Stones. Though perhaps he'd leave the attic till morning (not that he believed in ghosts or anything).

First up though, a trip to the studio to find those keys; then think of something to say to his aunt: *Wow! Amazing! You're so talented,* that kind of rubbish. Next job would be to get her out of the studio and rummage through her bag: *Very cold tonight, isn't it? Mind if I have an extra blanket and a hot water bottle?* Might even get chance to pinch a bit more cake.

Amelie opened the little walnut cupboard next to Storm's chair and a dozen DVDs and old videos tumbled out in a heap on the rug.

'I see you've got the latest *Harry Potter!*' Isla said. 'I haven't watched that one yet.'

Tim wanted *Spider-Man* but after much discussion they all settled on *Star Wars.*

'Are you sure, Isla? This one's quite old, you know, from

the seventies,' Amelie said. 'It's called *A New Hope.*'

'Sounds okay to me.'

'Our dad's favourite film,' Tim said quietly, thinking what a pity it was he couldn't actually remember him. He was just a name: Michael, or Dad. Somehow though, he could imagine him now, sitting on the floor beside them.

'I'd love to travel in space, wouldn't you?' said Isla.

Probably not, thought Amelie, but what an amazing theme that would be for Wild Billy Storm's book.

They all agreed how peaceful it was with Magnus gone.

'I hope he's not getting up to anything in the study,' Tim said. 'Storm must know what he's doing, I suppose. But all the same...'

'Yes,' said Amelie but her mind was elsewhere, preoccupied with all the strange things that had happened that day; first Dorin, then the Commander. 'What a weird day it's been.'

Isla nodded. 'Auntie George saw those lights, you know; Dad too on his way home from work.'

'I do wish I had.' Amelie had mind-wandered back to Cloud Hill where she'd glanced over her shoulder and seen the rainbow, a little sign of hope. 'At least I saw the Commander, I suppose.'

Later that night the wind died down and the skies began to clear. Amelie stood at her bedroom window, watching the moon and not knowing that Isla and Tim were doing exactly the same. A bright light streaked across the sky; a shooting star perhaps, and at once a warm blanket of reassurance wrapped itself around her; just as it had before.

She fished out her little crystal and held it up to the moonlight. Beams of light shone from it – gold and silver and the brightest blue. How could the world possibly end while something as beautiful as this existed?

'*A New Hope,*' she whispered, and closed her eyes to make a big wish.

Chapter Twelve
Storm's Revenge

The next morning, sunlight was already drying up the puddles, with little sign of the Weather Man's "deepening lows and vigorous depressions". The children rose early, eager to make the most of the good weather and visit their favourite cove.

'Summer's here at last.' Tim tapped sharply on Amelie's door. 'Are you awake?'

'Okay, no need to shout, I'm ready...' Amelie appeared, looking distinctly unready with her toothbrush in one hand and a hairbrush in the other.

'You look terrible!'

'Shut up, Tim, I'm tired. I was awake till gone midnight, finishing *Wild Billy Storm's Adventures in Outer Space*. He was rescued by aliens; nice aliens though, not ones who abducted you to Mars.'

'But Storm hasn't ever been rescued by aliens,' Tim said sensibly.

Amelie yawned. 'Well, he may have been for all you know. Anyway, that's the first chapter done. I woke up just now to find the bedside light on and my rainbow pen still in my hand...' And her little crystal in the other (but she left that bit out).

Just then Isla arrived, carrying her overnight bag and

a towel for the beach. 'Hey, I had such a funny dream last night. We all heard music playing on the old gramophone and your Aunt Eggy turned up in her beautiful gown with loads of other people, clapping and cheering. Then, out of the blue, this incredibly tall man appeared and loads of fifty dollar bills started to fall from the chandeliers…'

Was he the only one who hadn't seen the Commander, Tim wondered, taking the stairs two at a time…?

'Did you have a dream, Tim?' Isla asked, catching him up.

'No, I never remember dreams,' he lied. It wasn't really something he wanted to talk about. He'd been sitting in a train at Havenbridge Junction, waiting to go on a very long journey to visit his dad. All the model people in the little railway tin had come alive, including the portly station master who was getting very angry, blowing his whistle so loudly it hurt his ears. Once he spotted Tim he laughed raucously and ordered him off the train. 'Heaven? We don't go *there*, you idiot!'

He'd woken up feeling horribly troubled and sad. It felt like his dad was still waiting for him at the other end of the line… But only now did it dawn on him: the station master was Magnus. 'Well, let's hope your dream comes true anyway, Isla,' he said, 'we could certainly do with those fifty dollar bills.'

'I hope so too. Shall we give Magnus a shout?'

'Are you mad? He'll be down there already, never last in the queue for food.'

They burst into the kitchen, their appetites kindled by the smell of fried eggs and tomatoes and toast. But to their surprise, there was no sign of Magnus. Just Storm, immersed in his morning paper, and Lucy with her back to the window; looking, they noticed, extremely annoyed.

'A fine start to the holiday this is!' she said.

Amelie's heart sank. Her report had arrived already!

'Yeah,' said Tim breezily. 'Summer at last! We're off to the beach…'

'You're not going anywhere till I find out what happened.'

'Happened?' Amelie and Tom choroused in shared bewilderment. There was Magnus's empty seat and a rack of fresh toast, as yet untouched. 'Where is he?'

'You know perfectly well! And if one of you doesn't own up you'll be grounded…'

'What?' Tim protested. 'You are joking!'

'So who did it then?'

'Did what exactly?'

'Scared the wits out of Magnus…'

Amelie let out a grateful sigh; at least she was safe for now.

'We haven't,' Tim insisted, 'more's the pity though. Ask Isla.'

Isla nodded. 'Tim's right, Auntie Lucy; I was with them all evening. He sneaked off to watch *Curse of the Dark Hearts*.'

'There you go!' Tim sat down in a huff and poured milk on his cornflakes.

Storm, quite oblivious to the unfolding drama, absently sprinkled salt on his porridge.

'Fine by me,' said Amelie, helping herself to a big squirt of tomato ketchup. 'I don't care if I'm grounded. I can finish my novel instead. Here…' She passed Isla a plate.

'Well, I mind,' Tim objected and shot an accusing glance at his mother. 'What has Magnus being late for breakfast got to do with us anyway?'

'He's not late, Timothy. But, as you can see, he's not *here*.'

'You mean he's gone?' Amelie's imagination was immediately sparked. 'Magnus – abducted, you mean?'

Tim choked on his toast. 'Who'd want to abduct Magnus?'

But Amelie could already see the Commander heaving Magnus off to Havenbridge Woods in a big wheelbarrow to teach him a lesson.

'Have you tried the garden?' Isla suggested, trying to be practical. 'It's a lovely morning.'

'Magnus miss breakfast? I don't think so.' Amelie took two extra slices of toast, just in case he returned. She looked out of the kitchen window. 'Looks like there'll be a hot spell, after all.'

Storm had now finished his porridge and was engrossed in his paper once more, muttering about the state of the world. He sipped his tea absently, spilling most of it down his pullover. Amelie gazed at him thoughtfully. She couldn't imagine ever being old. She was going to stay a child forever and never grow up, not past thirteen anyway, and that was less than three years away.

'What smell?' Storm asked vaguely, dabbing his chin with a napkin, his mind still pondering the day's latest news. 'Vicar's still in shock then, poor chap.' He chuckled to himself. Those *Strange Lights over Havenbridge* had finally caught up with the vicar, sending out a force so strong it nearly knocked him off his bike. 'Probes,' he murmured. 'Remarkable things... Hah! I can just see Mrs Jolley pouring him a strong cup of tea, laced with a drop of brandy to calm his nerves, eh, Lucy?'

But Lucy wasn't listening. 'Magnus went home, and I'm certain you two know why. Something happened last night, so disturbing he's refusing to speak about it. And Mona swears it's all *your* doing - and blames *me* for not taking proper care of him.'

'As if!' Tim snorted. 'It's that horror film, I'm telling you. His fault for not watching *Star Wars* with us...'

For some reason a terror-stricken Magnus had called for a taxi in the early hours, then climbed out of the study window, and run down the drive.

'He arrived home in his pyjamas with his hair standing on end. The party was in full swing and Mona and Maynard's night was completely ruined.'

'Ruined!' Tim spluttered. 'Magnus turning up in his pyjamas? I bet they all wet themselves. I would have.'

Amelie's green eyes shone. 'So it was him then - the Commander!' In her excitement, the words slipped out. 'No wonder he was so scared!'

'Commander? What on earth are you talking about now, Amelie?' Lucy said crossly.

'The tall man on the stairs,' Amelie began but then Storm looked up, grinning like a naughty schoolboy. He was holding his magnifying glass close to one eye which made it look twice as big as the other. It was all Isla could do not to giggle.

'Hah! I'm afraid it was me, Lucy,' he roared. 'I'm the guilty party. Are you going to ground me too? It all began with that story...' One Magnus had listened to rather too carefully, he quickly explained.

Shortly after he'd left them all that evening Storm happened to spot Magnus on his way to the studio. 'To see you for some unknown reason, dear Lucy...'

For years he'd wanted to teach the brat a lesson and now was his chance! With Magnus safely out of the way, he'd crept into his study and found a small glass paperweight in a drawer. This he placed inside a little wooden box with a handwritten note: *Confidential: property of Eglantyne Marigold Trott*, then tucked it in an unlocked drawer in the roll-top desk. He'd paused there a moment to admire a little hand-painted figure he'd stored there long ago.

'A model of Yoda, the Jedi Master in Star Wars,' he said fondly, 'one your father made when he was no older than you, Tim.'

'I remember that one,' Tim said.

Storm continued. He'd set his alarm clock for two thirty in the morning and sat reading a while before finally falling asleep. Then, when the alarm roused him as planned, he climbed out of bed, pulled on his dressing gown and threw an old blackout curtain over his head. He crept outside and waited in the dark hallway, shone a torch under the study door, flashing its light on and off. Then, getting no response, he made a few tapping noises with his stick. When finally Magnus opened the door a terrible, luminous face stared back at him in the dark.

'Honestly, Storm, how could you!' Lucy said, covering her smile with her hands.

'Nice one, Storm!' Tim laughed. 'Though we were a bit worried about Eggy's Stone.'

'Don't worry, that's locked away safely,' the old man chuckled. 'But needless to say, he pinched my old glass paperweight instead.'

Amelie gazed at him in wonder. 'But how did you make it *loonymus*?'

'Don't tell me you've forgotten! The old curtain had a luminous face painted on it already, something I did one Halloween to amuse you. Anyway,' he continued, 'since Magnus didn't believe in ghosts, I thought I might broaden his mind.' He began to chuckle again. 'Therefore, I affected a high-pitched voice... like this: *It's mine! It's mine! Give me my Stone of Power!*'

Isla said she wished she had a grandfather like Storm; someone who played tricks and flew airplanes.

'Well, when I was a boy we had to make our own entertainment, Isla,' Storm reminisced. 'No television, just the wireless, so playing tricks became a favourite pastime.'

'Wow, you even had *wireless* back then, Mr Trott? I thought computers weren't invented then.'

'No, no, it's what we called the radio in those days.'

'I wish I'd seen Magnus's face!' Amelie planted a kiss on his cheek. 'You're so cool, Storm! Magnus's *menesis*; like Darth Vader in Star Wars...'

'*Nemesis*,' Isla whispered.

'That's what I said.'

'What on earth will you think of us, Isla?' tutted Lucy, even though Isla promised it was the funniest thing she'd ever heard. 'Good, but now what do I tell Mona and Maynard, Storm?'

'That their son is an insufferable oik, my dear. And you might mention he's stolen a glass paperweight from my desk.' He slapped his hand down on the table to show that the subject was now closed, and returned to his newspaper.

After breakfast they planned to go to the beach but not before they had shown Isla the garden.

'You two go on ahead and I'll make us a picnic for the beach,' Tim said helpfully.

Lucy smiled. 'I should have believed you,' she said, ruffling his hair affectionately. 'You get off then and have a lovely day.'

'Thanks Tim,' Amelie said, 'and I'll show Isla the hangar since she's going to be a pilot.'

Lara bounded after them, followed by Freddie, who got a little distracted on the way, chasing butterflies. Finally, along came Storm, carefully avoiding snails on the path, and tottering after them in his sunhat and an old tweed jacket with a radiant smile on his face.

Chapter Thirteen

The Earth Watchers

The postman came whistling up the drive and left a handful of letters on the kitchen table.

'Lovely day, Mrs Trott, just what we need. Kids off down the beach? Give you a bit of peace...'

'Thank you, Sam, hope you've brought me something nice for a change.' Lucy made herself a large mug of coffee, pulled on her artist's smock and wandered into the dining room to open the post. More bills, two warning letters from the bank; and another she would look at later. She tossed them all onto the mountain of post already littering the table and wandered through to her studio.

'Michael, tell me, what do I do now?' she said, sinking down in her favourite chair.

'Keep painting, my love!' the man in the portrait replied, as clearly as if he were right there in the room.

That was all: 'Keep painting!' As though nothing else in this world really mattered. Not even losing their home.

She picked up her brushes and palette and sat by an empty canvas by the window where, gazing out at the sunlit garden, she was rewarded with the most beautiful sight.

Hadleigh House garden was a little overgrown today but the rain had created a bright green paradise. Trees, bushes and grass all sparkled in the morning light. The surrounding pastureland was bathed in a haze of heat, and in the distance, a little flock of sheep and a family of horses from a nearby farm grazed happily in the unexpected warmth.

Amelie and Isla scrambled through the tangled grass and stopped briefly at the playhouse to drop off their things. It was full of spiders and smelled strongly of damp.

'Tim said to open the windows and let the sun dry it out,' Amelie said. 'It really needs a good clean but not today; tomorrow maybe.'

They continued along the path and came to a little footbridge that crossed the stream. Here they flopped down while Lara leapt in and out of the water, soaking them both as she shook herself dry. Freddie rolled over in the sunlight as though he'd never seen summer before.

Eventually, they got up and headed towards a little half-hidden rose garden that Storm had dedicated to Louisa. Its flowers were in full bloom and still wet with dew; they fingered the petals gently then strolled on through the great orchard where an archway of ancient pear trees and apple trees showered them as they ducked beneath their branches.

At the far end of the garden was the hangar.

'Storm's on his way,' Tim said, running up the path behind them. 'The hangar opens out to acres of fields, Isla.'

'Great runway,' she observed.

Meanwhile, Storm paused to survey his vegetable patch. It certainly needed some attention but would wait another day.

'What do you think then, Isla?' he said, catching up with them in the hangar at last. He opened the door and removed a grubby old tarpaulin to expose a small, rather delicate looking flying machine with shiny red wings and two red seats.

He stroked the little aircraft proudly. 'I built this myself.'

'Mr Trott, it's amazing! I'd love to learn how to fly this. Can I sit in it, please?'

'But of course. And call me Storm, for pity's sake, girl. Maybe we'll have a trip in her one of these days.' He hadn't flown the little aircraft for thirty years and it was his dearest wish to have one more flight. 'Here, take this with you.' He took down a dusty looking book from the shelf where he kept all his tools.

'A flying manual!' Isla's face was alight with excitement. 'I'll read it tonight.'

'Storm,' said Tim with a serious look on his face, 'we've got something important to ask you…'

A loud squeal emitted from Storm's ear as he adjusted his hearing device. 'Fire away then, lad!'

'Who were those people who saved you?'

The old man paused and looked up at the sky. 'The Earth Watchers, you mean?'

'Earth Watchers…?' The three children stared at him quizzically.

'They're a group of very advanced individuals from afar; very advanced indeed.'

Isla nodded thoughtfully. 'You mean other planets, don't you?' Something very out of the ordinary was going on here and with only a few weeks before she left for Washington she really didn't want to miss out. 'How do you know all this stuff, Mr Trott? I mean Storm,' she corrected herself.

'Well, my Aunt Eglantyne first met them in 1914 just before the start of the First World War, then again in the 1920s during her travels to South America and the Far East. She was the first in our family to have any contact with the Earth Watchers though I was probably the only one at the time who believed her.'

'I wish I'd known Aunt Eggy,' Amelie said. 'I'd have believed her.'

'Well, you're so very like her, my dear.' Storm ruffled her hair. 'Even though…'

'Even though what?' Amelie waited for him to continue

but he carried on talking instead:

'They came again to Havenbridge in the summer of 1939, shortly before the outbreak of World War Two; lights began to appear in the sky, with unexplained sightings of a very tall man...' He winked at Amelie. 'All sounding rather familiar, eh? And then there were the 1960s, of course, when the world was dangerously close to war once more.'

'But we're not at war now,' Tim said.

'Nor are we at peace, Tim,' the old man said gravely. 'We have deadly weapons being tested and lunatics in power. Not a good combination. Keep watching for signs!'

'Like those balls of light that followed the vicar and Sergeant Buggley?'

'Exactly, Amelie.'

Amelie nodded solemnly. 'Isla even had a dream about him.'

'Yes, they'll often appear in our dreams.' He smiled. 'And you know how important mind-wandering is.'

'Is it a good sign when they do?' Isla asked.

Storm did not answer at once. 'Good and bad,' he said eventually. 'Good because they only ever come to help us but bad because danger is usually...'

'Imminent?'

'I'm afraid so, Isla; it would appear that danger is very close indeed.'

Amelie's eyes brimmed with tears. 'We're going to lose our home, aren't we?'

'Let's hope not, Amelie; anyway, I suspect there's something even greater at stake.' He put an arm around her shoulder. 'Though perhaps you're half right... Because of our family's long association with the Earth Watchers, they'll often turn up during times of personal distress.' He swallowed hard, remembering how they had come to comfort him after That Terrible Day.

'You mean,' Tim said, 'they have the power to save

Hadleigh?'

'They always do what they can, Tim. They saved my life, after all. However, they're not permitted to interfere with our destiny. That will always be down to us.' He turned to leave. 'Try not to worry, my dears. But do keep watching for signs…'

'I'll come with you, Storm,' Amelie said, linking his arm. 'I'll see you two back at the playhouse in a bit.'

Tim and Isla remained in the hangar, taking turns in the pilot's seat and studying the controls in the microlight manual.

'Does Mum know about the Earth Watchers?' she asked Storm as they wandered back to the house. 'I haven't told her about the Commander yet but it sounds like she caught a glimpse of him on the stairs. At least I told you though.'

He smiled and patted her hand affectionately. 'You can tell me anything, anytime, you know that. Your dad knew all about them, of course; he loved my stories as a boy. Unfortunately, your mother remains a little, shall we say, sceptical?'

Amelie looked up at him and sighed. 'Storm, do you think I'm odd?'

'No, of course not, my dear.'

'It's just that I hate being different. I don't seem to fit in with the rest of the world and I've only got you and Isla for friends…'

'Different? But of course you're different, my love! There's no one quite like you - never has been and never will be. And that's how it's meant to be. We're all perfectly different…'

'I suppose.' Amelie gazed up at the cloudless sky. 'Do you think we're alone in the universe, Storm?'

'Just us?' He paused at the kitchen door and laughed. 'Good Lord, no! What a terrible waste of space that would be!' Then, hearing a noise they wandered round to the front of the house.

Eli Dankstone was there with huge ladders that reached up to the chimneys. In the back of his van was a big sack filled with old tiles. They looked up and watched him, chipping away at the roof. The old house looked so shabby and sad. Paint had begun to peel from the window frames, gutters were broken.

Amelie's head had begun to fill up with more doubts. It's all so impossible, she thought sadly, remembering her own uncertain future at school. Even the thought of Dorin and the Commander, or her writing a best-selling book didn't help. Perhaps she'd just imagined it all, after all. Everything was falling apart.

'Amelie,' her great-grandfather said kindly, 'never let any little wretched voice of doubt trouble you. And don't forget I have this…'

She glanced up at him with tears in her eyes as he took the mysterious Stone of Power from his pocket and held it up to the light. 'I can safely show you this now Magnus has gone.'

Amelie gazed at it in awe; it was just like her own!

'It's been my protection for more than seventy years and has never failed me yet.'

#

Magnus Bottomley-Sligh was still on his second breakfast when he recalled the events of the night before. He helped himself to another plateful of bacon, trying to forget what he'd witnessed. At least he had the Stone; that was worth three more sausages and an extra-large slice of fried bread.

'Poor Nussy has had such a terrible shock,' his mother crooned. 'He needs feeding up.'

Maynard Bottomley-Sligh grunted. 'Has he got the ruddy keys though?'

Mona ignored him. 'Why don't you tell us what those

hateful children did? They've always had it in for you. I'll have them put in care; a home for delinquents.'

Magnus brightened, cheered by the thought of them all locked away.

'Yes, Mona. They even tried to steal my new phone in the middle of the night while I was asleep.' He stuffed another sausage into his mouth and pretended to cry.

'No wonder you came home so upset, sweetie...'

'Where are the keys, you great lummox?' Maynard persisted. 'We can't do much till we have them.'

'Don't call poor Nussy that,' Mona chided, stroking Magnus's bulging cheek. 'Here, try some chocolate muffins...'

'I did much better than keys!' Magnus spluttered with pride and forced a whole muffin into his mouth. 'I got a Stone of Power!'

He'd rooted around in old Storm's study and sat on the big swivel chair, searching through drawers full of old batteries, shirt buttons, broken spectacles and oh, how gross, a pair of false teeth, until finally he came upon a little wooden box. It wasn't even locked! There was a note inside, and a round, shiny object that might have been mistaken for a piece of glass had he not known better. 'It was so powerful it buzzed in my hands.' He could hear old Storm snoring loudly next door so, since he'd had no luck as yet with the keys, he decided to chance his luck and nick the other Stone of Power too.

He crept into the hall and tentatively tried Storm's door. It was locked. Never mind, he'd wake him later; tell him he could smell smoke (that'd get him out of the way!) then nip in and grab his trousers.

But things didn't quite go to plan. Back in the study he dozed off for a while until a bright light suddenly roused him. It came from beneath the door, followed by a strange tapping sound. The rest he couldn't bear to remember so he reached for another chocolate muffin.

'Yes, you eat up, poppet,' his mother simpered.

Maynard's eyes narrowed. 'Show me!'

Magnus reached into his dressing gown pocket and slowly opened his hand to reveal his treasure. But before he could clamp his fingers around it a purple-faced Maynard seized it and threw it across the room.

'That's mine, Maynard!' Magnus wailed. 'Give me my Stone of Power!'

'It's a ruddy bit of glass, you fool!' his father exploded. 'Old Storm's set you up – and after all I've taught you!'

'No, no, you don't understand; that's what *he* said: it *looks* like glass but it isn't.'

'Mona, the useless brat's been conned. Storm's up to his tricks again. Phone Eli now and tell him to do his worst. We'll have those Trotts out of there in no time at all!'

Chapter Fourteen

A Grim Encounter in Devil's Gulley

By mid-morning the beach had become quite busy. The first of the holiday makers had already arrived: surfers carrying boards, families with squealing children and noisy dogs in tow; retired couples armed with blankets and folding chairs.

'I'm glad we didn't leave it much later,' said Tim, spreading a brightly coloured beach towel on the sand. 'Here's just perfect with the dunes as a windbreak.' He hid their picnic bag behind a rock and took out a tube of sunscreen which he passed around.

'Even I need this, you know,' Isla laughed, rubbing cream on her conker-brown arms. 'Here, Amelie, you need it the most...'

They sat down and gazed out to sea, watching the breakers as the tide came in, and breathing in the delicious summer scents of seaweed and suntan oil.

Soon, a group of Year Ten boys from school spotted them. One of them was carrying a football.

'Hey, Tim – wanna game, mate?'

Tim ran over to join them then looked back and whistled through his teeth to Isla. 'You fancy a game too?'

Isla sauntered over with Lara, swiftly intercepted the ball, dribbled a while then passed it with one strong kick to Tim who scored a goal.

Amelie sat cross-legged on a beach towel, lazily soaking up the warmth. She watched proudly as one of the boys stopped in his tracks.

'Hey, she's good for a girl!'

'I'm good, period,' Isla laughed.

It was a blissful day; one they each vowed they'd never forget. They swam and played tag on the sand, feasted on Tim's peanut butter sandwiches and potato crisps, and rounded it all off with a banana and a Mars bar each and a bottle of Storm's homemade lemonade.

Lara enjoyed her customary dip in the sea but Freddie curled up on a small blanket they'd taken expressly since he didn't much like getting sand in his paws. And all the while, Amelie kept her little crystal close, safely zipped inside the pocket of her shorts.

At six o'clock, they packed up their things. The sea air had sharpened their appetites and made them quite drowsy. It was a warm evening with no more than a gentle breeze so they took a detour and strolled down to the harbour to buy ice-creams before heading back to Cloud Cottage with Isla.

All of a sudden, Lara became very excited and Tim had to put her back on the lead. 'What's up, you silly dog?'

She let out three loud, insistent yelps, then ran in circles and got herself tangled up in her lead. Freddie, who had draped himself around Amelie's shoulder, peered up at the sky and began to chatter like he did when he saw birds, not that he had ever caught one in his life.

Mystified, the three children put down their bags. Looking up, they shaded their eyes, only to see a flock of noisy young seagulls trying out their wings.

'Look!' Tim shouted. 'Up there – Chinese lanterns...' They were now flying directly above them, in little groups of three, heading north. 'There must be a party going on somewhere.' As soon as he'd said it he knew it couldn't be true. He'd had a strange feeling the moment he saw them;

almost as though, whatever those lights really were, someone was watching them and trying to get their attention. And indeed they now had, thanks to Freddie and Lara.

'How amazing is that!' Amelie felt unbelievably light, as though her feet had just left the ground. She understood now what people meant by walking on air!

'See how fast they're moving,' Isla said, 'far too fast for lanterns. When I get home I'll ask Dad.' She glanced at her watch. It was nearly seven o'clock. 'Speaking of which, I'd better head back.'

When they reached Cloud Cottage Tim and Amelie waved her goodbye but neither of them felt much like going home just yet. After so many weeks of rain it was good to enjoy some evening sun. Tim handed Amelie Lara's lead and lifted Freddie onto his shoulder. 'Why don't we take these two back, have a quick bite to eat and come out again? You never know, we might catch some more of those lights.'

Their mother was still busy in her studio when they returned. She had flung open the French windows and was sitting with a paintbrush between her teeth, assessing her latest work. Hearing them, she turned and smiled; a look of relief on her face.

'I'm so pleased to see you back, safe and sound.'

'We're not late, are we?'

She shook her head. 'No, no, it's just been so quiet without you. I've missed your chatter…'

The truth was she had begun to feel a little uneasy. Her first thought was the children, of course. And though she may have imagined it again she could have sworn she'd seen that giant of a man on the stairs just now.

Tim came over to view her new painting. 'Whoa, that's amazing, Mum! Is tea ready though? We're starving.'

'Yes,' she laughed, 'jacket potatoes keeping warm in the oven; salad in the fridge and there's some left-over pizza too.' She picked up a fine brush and began to add a small detail or two to her painting. 'Looks like Magnus had most of the cake.'

'Pig!' said Amelie. 'We should never have let him come. What's happened with the roof then, Mum? There were loads of broken tiles in the back of Eli Dankstone's van this morning.'

'He's mended what he can but we won't really know till it rains again. I'm just waiting for his bill now. Done his best, I think...'

'Worst, more like,' Amelie murmured, thinking of the broken tiles. She rested her chin on her mother's head, and tried to put her uncertainties aside. Her gaze fell upon her father's portrait. Hello Dad, she said silently, Mum's lonely, you know. I do wish I could make her happy. Would you mind too much if she met someone new?

'I really love your new painting, Mum. Those patterns of light on the playhouse wall are amazing. What are they?' It was such an unusual picture, quite unlike anything she'd ever seen before.

'I've no idea, love; they've gone now the sun has moved to the west. They appeared soon after you left this morning. Look, I took a few photos...' She reached for her phone. 'See that?'

There they were - little crosses and circles of light on the playhouse walls, and yet more on the path leading down to the stream. Maybe they were the kind of signs Storm meant. 'We saw some Chinese lanterns earlier.'

'Lanterns? I doubt it - the council banned them last year. They caused an awful lot of trouble for the coastguards who confused them with distress signals at sea. Not to mention the harm they were doing to wild life.'

Tim returned with a huge wedge of pizza in his hand. 'Okay if we go out for a bit, Mum?'

'What, again?' Then reluctantly, seeing the disappointment on their faces: 'Well, as it's the holidays, yes. But I want you home well before dark, half nine at the latest. You're in charge, Tim.'

They wolfed down their tea and wandered back to the harbour.

'I'm still hungry,' Tim said, 'but I found a bit of change in my room, enough to share a bag of chips.'

They stopped off at Gina's Chippy and sat on the harbour wall, eating their chips and watching the boats bobbing at anchor in the still waters. It was a while before either of them spoke; as though time itself had dropped anchor too.

'It feels odd without Isla, doesn't it?' Amelie said at last.

Tim nodded. 'We've got half an hour before we need to turn back. Let's go round by the public gardens. They'll be open till late.'

There was a little play area there with swings and a climbing frame. They took it in turns on the swings, flying so high it took their breath away; their laughter piercing the quiet evening air. Another few days and the gardens and beaches would be overrun with more holiday makers. It was good to have it all to themselves for a while.

By the time they left the gardens it was almost dusk, so Tim suggested they take a shortcut through Devil's Gulley, between the Hearts of Oak pub and the fishing tackle shop. It was always a bit rowdy at this end of town with men arguing over their pints of beer or singing noisily to the juke box in the pub, but at least they would make it home on time.

'I really don't like it here,' Amelie whispered. Her hand tightened around the little stone in her pocket. She would never have dared to walk through the Gulley alone, even in daytime, and though she knew she was safe with Tim she still sensed danger close by. One of the problems of being a writer and having an overactive imagination, Tim teased.

'Almost there,' he added reassuringly. Shadows fell across their path but soon the streetlights appeared. Then, just before they stepped out into the High Street, a dark figure loomed over them. Amelie sneezed.

Eli Dankstone. He leered and blew smoke in their faces; his gold teeth glinted in the light from the street lamp. 'So, the lady of the house again!' He drew closer and with a menacing look in his eyes squeezed Amelie's arm; so hard she almost let out a yell. 'Well, well, young Master Trott too; I had a feeling I'd see you.' He reeked of beer and stale cigarettes. 'You'd better "trot" off then, hadn't you?' With this he let out a raucous laugh. 'Go on, trot, trot! Anything could happen at this time of night.' It sounded more like a threat than concern for their welfare. He laughed again and slunk back against the wall.

'Ignore him.' Tim grasped Amelie's wrist and they hurried out into the High Street and on to Primrose Lane before turning up Cloud Hill to Hadleigh House. 'I wish we'd got that Stone of Power,' he said.

At last they were home. Breathless, Amelie flung open the door and caught her reflection in the mirror. Despite their day at the beach all the colour had drained from her cheeks. She rubbed her arm. There was even a nasty bruise where he'd grabbed her. She searched Tim's face anxiously. 'It felt like he was lying in wait.'

'Forget him. I'm much more interested in those lights earlier.'

'They weren't lanterns at all, were they, Tim? Do you think they were Storm's Earth Watcher friends?'

Tim nodded slowly. 'Watching us.'

'You mean spying on us?'

'Not in a bad way. Like Storm says, they're only here to help.'

'And warn us, you think?'

Tim yawned. 'Let's see what tomorrow brings.' He went to the window and spotted a shadowy figure disappearing quickly down the drive. He was pretty sure it was Eli

Dankstone though there was no way he'd tell Amelie that.

Isla's father had just been called out on an emergency so she didn't get chance to ask him about the lanterns, and Auntie George was busy on the phone. She switched on her laptop and waited. Anyway, she reminded herself, she'd seen Chinese lanterns before and those lights definitely weren't the same thing at all. '*Unusual Lights… flying over Havenbridge… 7 pm tonight;* let's see what this brings up…'

The screen was soon filled with reports of similar sightings from all over the country. Some were local; bright lights seen near the coast, others further inland, even as far north as London, some fifty miles away.

How her life had changed since she'd met Amelie and Tim. She reached into her overnight bag for Storm's flying manual. What a great bedtime read that would be!

Back at Hadleigh House, Lucy Trott checked all the downstairs windows, then switched off the lights and went into the hallway to bolt the front door. The animals were fed, the children now safely in bed, and old Storm had gone to his room. She sat for a moment at the foot of the stairs and closed her eyes. At least with no rain their roof would be safe for a while. Tomorrow was another day.

Just as she was about to climb the stairs, she spotted a white envelope on the mat. How odd, the postman always brought letters to the back. Intrigued, she stooped to retrieve it and slitting it open with her thumbnail, began to read. Then, hearing a sound, she looked up, and there was the very tall man once more.

Chapter Fifteen
A Family Conference

'Family Conference?' Amelie lifted a piece of toast and honey to her mouth and paused. 'What for?' she asked suspiciously. 'And can Isla come too? She's family too, after all.'

'Not this time, Amelie. But you can explain to her later.'

Amelie and Tim exchanged glances. Family Conferences were only ever called when important decisions had to be made – like how to celebrate Storm's birthday, or draw up a new rota for the washing up.

It's my school report, Amelie decided miserably. Either I'm to have extra lessons in the holidays or I've been thrown out of school.

'It's the house,' Tim said, fearing the worst.

'Finish your breakfast, Tim. I need to make a few telephone calls first and then we'll talk later. Eleven o'clock, and don't be late.'

Outside the sun was shining. More patterns of light had appeared on the footpath, just like the ones in their mother's painting. Amelie ran on ahead.

'Look, there are more on our playhouse!'

'Earth Watchers, I bet.' Tim took out his mobile phone to photograph them. 'Now, we've got our very own record.' He opened the playhouse door and carried a small table and a rickety chair outside. 'Let's do something useful while we're waiting. Pass me the yard brush, will you?'

While Tim swept the floor, Amelie absently flicked away cobwebs with an old towel. But her mind was busy elsewhere: fretting over her school report, and all the trouble she was in. Then she remembered the little crystal in her pocket.

'There,' she said brightly. 'Look how much bigger it is now it's all clean and tidy. Maybe a few cushions for the sofa and some flowers for the table though. I'll see what I can find.'

She left Tim cleaning the windows and returned later with a couple of old cushions, a potted geranium, and a string of solar-powered lights. 'Let me untangle these...' She sat patiently threading them this way and that until finally... 'There, that's better. I'll hang these around the door.'

'Cool!' Tim stood back to admire their work. 'Hey, it's nearly eleven already and I can see Storm waving from the kitchen window.'

They assembled around the kitchen table and their mother began to shuffle a few papers in front of her. 'I'll get straight to the point.' She held up a white envelope. 'Last night I received this report...'

'I knew it.' Amelie held her breath. 'What's going to happen to me, Mum?'

Her mother raised an eyebrow in surprise. '*You*, Amelie? I'm afraid this concerns all of us. Things are rather worse than I thought.'

She opened the envelope and placed the report on the table. Storm picked it up at once, frowned, and stirred an extra spoonful of sugar into his coffee to sweeten his mood. It was headed *Elias Dankstone and Co.* He shook his head and passed it to Tim.

'What about me?' Amelie frowned. 'Don't I get to see it?'

'Here,' Tim glanced at it and passed it to her. 'I knew it

was him, creeping around here last night!'

Amelie studied the report. Hadleigh House needed urgent re-wiring; dry rot was destroying the floorboards and wet rot the rafters. A new damp course was required, plus a new roof, a new boiler, new windows; and so the list went on.

'And remind me how much that little lot will cost?' Storm said dryly.

'£33,800 apparently, plus whatever he's done so far…'

He whistled. 'Exactly, daylight robbery!'

'I hate him!' Amelie rested her elbows on the table, chin in her hands. 'He's after the tunnels.'

'Or the land to build on,' Tim said. 'It's all a big scam to trick us into selling up. I reckon Maynard's paying him, don't you? To make things look worse than they really are.'

'All the same,' Lucy pointed out, 'the roof is leaking, and we do need a new boiler and windows too; not to mention the damp everywhere. Our insurance won't cover it all so even without Elias Dankstone we'd have to find £15,000 just for the roof. And that's without all our bills piling up.' She turned to Storm who was watching her over the top of his spectacles. 'Storm, we may have no choice. Hadleigh is just too big for us now.'

'No choice? What exactly are you saying, Lucy Trott?'

'Oh, no, we can't move!' Amelie blurted, fighting back her tears. 'Not ever! I'll ask Charlie, he knows loads of people. Anyone is better than Eli Dankstone.'

'Yes,' Tim said, 'we'll even go without pocket money, and birthday and Christmas presents; but no, we're *not* moving…'

'Tim darling, your pocket money is a mere drop in the ocean. You see, even if I worked all day and all night I could never make enough money to run this house. We have barely enough to live on as it is.'

'What about the Stones of Power, Storm?' Amelie said.

'Wouldn't they help?'

'Please, Amelie!' her mother snapped, 'I'm in no mood for that rubbish.'

'Or the tunnels?' Tim said. 'Supposing there really is gold hidden there?'

'Stop it, Tim, this nonsense really isn't helping.'

Storm reached out and patted Amelie's hand. 'No, my dear, I'm afraid those Stones aren't sources of material wealth. And as for the tunnels, they were sealed off years ago.'

'Well, if it's gold the Bottomley-Slighs are so interested in, why don't we just tell them the truth?'

'Because they're driven by greed and superstition; they'd never believe truth if it stared them in the face.' The old man stirred his coffee soberly. 'Gold apart, they'd no doubt want to use the tunnels for their own nefarious business.'

'*Nofairyus*?' Amelie said. 'Let me write that down. That means evil, doesn't it?'

'Yes,' Storm said grimly. 'Well, we have to raise that money somehow. Now, if only Eggy's diaries were to come to light...'

Amelie had suddenly become very quiet. She sat, concentrating fiercely on the little crystal in her pocket with a very strange look on her face.

'We could sell a rug or two,' continued Storm, 'and a couple of Eggy's wall hangings. They'd maybe fetch a few thousand. Other than that, we have no assets remaining. This house is literally all we have.'

'Don't worry, we'll think of something.' Tim put a comforting arm around his sister's shoulder but her face had already relaxed into a smile. The little crystal had done its work. Her green eyes sparkled as she turned to him. 'I think we may have the answer already, Tim...' She placed a hand on her mother's arm: 'Don't you worry either, Mum. In fact, don't do *anything* just yet. Give me two weeks, that's all, and I promise you everything will work out fine...'

The two children wandered outside to reflect on the news just as Isla was coming up the drive on her bicycle.

'We need another conference,' Amelie said. 'But just us: you, me, and Isla. Right, you two go to the playhouse, I need to fetch a few things first.'

'How beautiful it all looks,' Isla said. The door and windows had been strung with Amelie's fairy lights. She ran her hand over the outside walls. 'And look at these light patterns too. These are a sign of hope surely, like those lights we saw in the sky last night.'

'We certainly need some hope, Isla. We're about to lose our home. That's unless we can raise enough money to stop Mum selling. Anyway, Amelie's got some crazy idea so I suppose we should wait and see what it is.'

'If there's anything I can do to help...' Isla followed Tim inside and stopped abruptly. 'Hey, you've done wonders in here!' There were still a few spiders' webs here and there but it smelled a lot less musty now the sun had dried out the wood.

Amelie soon returned with a notebook and pen, and a pair of old spectacles that had once belonged to Storm. She handed out three sheets of lined paper, ripped out of her notebook.

'What's this?' Tim said, picking one up. 'Ajender'?

'I think it's meant to say Agenda,' Isla said.

'The *Ajender* is what our meeting is all about: *Operation Save Hadleigh House*.' Amelie pushed the rickety chair against the wall so it didn't collapse while she sat on it. 'I'm the Chair. I have to run the meeting because it was my idea.'

'In that case you need a proper chair to sit on. I'll go and get one.'

'Thank you, Tim,' Amelie said grandly. She took the old spectacles from their case and tried them on. 'Isla, you can take Minutes.'

'Minutes?'

'They're notes. Just write down everything we say. It's what our teachers do when they have meetings. I know. I had to stay behind one day for not paying attention in class and that's what they were doing. It was all so interesting I left all my work and had to stay behind all over again.'

'Here, this one is safe,' Tim said, returning with a garden chair. He settled down again to read his 'Ajender':

1 *Prescent*

2 *Aplogolys*

3 *A nofairyus situachon.*

4 *How to get lodes of muney*

5 *Any other busyness*

6 *Date of next meating*

'Right,' Amelie began. 'Tim, you'll be our treasurer because you're good with money.'

'Cheers, but we haven't got any money, have we?'

'No, but we will have soon. Wait till you hear my brilliant idea.' She lowered the spectacles to the tip of her nose.

'Fire away then!' Tim attempted to conceal a smile. 'Why have you got those things on the end of your nose?'

'Because I can't see otherwise,' she replied nonchalantly.

Tim looked at Isla. 'Best not to ask…'

'Ready now?' Amelie clapped her hands. 'Let's begin with our *nofairyus* situation. But before we do, Isla has to write down who's present.'

'Well, we do know who's present,' Isla pointed out. 'You, me and Tim…'

'I *know*.' Amelie sighed with what she hoped sounded like patience. 'But it's how it's done in meetings, Isla. And we mustn't forget the apologies either, that's people who are very sorry but they couldn't come for some reason. Put down Freddie and Lara; and Storm. Now, onto our evil situation…'

'We already know what our situation is,' Tim said, getting

restless. 'The Slighs are after our house and we'll soon be homeless. Let's move on to how to get loads of money.'

'Good. Well, that brings me to my brilliant idea.'

They would hold a Grand Ballroom Sale, she announced. Storm had given her the idea really, selling Eggy's oriental rugs and wall hangings. There were, as they knew, plenty of old clothes and bits of furniture, scattered around the house. In fact, more than enough stuff in the attic and Ballroom to fill a shop; and people loved buying old things. Look at all the antique shops in Havenbridge and Littlehaven, she reminded them.

'Vintage,' said Isla. 'It's very popular back home. What an awesome idea, Amelie.'

'And then there are my books. I've written two stories already. 'There's a printer in town. It won't cost much, I'm sure. I've found a jar full of five pence pieces under my bed, and Mum can design the covers.'

Tim looked dubious. 'If you think you can…'

'I *know* I can,' Amelie said robustly and was relieved to know that the Voice of Doubt had nothing to say.

'Then there's Mum's paintings,' Tim said, warming to the idea. 'And Storm has loads of antiquarian books…'

Amelie nodded. 'Those might interest Kenny Pratt in the fishing tackle shop.'

Tim concealed another smile. '*Antiquarian*, not aquarium, Amelie; like very old and rare books. But we'll ask Kenny anyway. We need everyone in Havenbridge to come.'

'Not everyone,' Amelie said darkly. 'Snarkey for one, or the Specks; they're her Secret Agents, Isla, and definitely not Eli Dankstone and the Bottomley-Slighs.'

'Of course…' They all nodded gravely.

Isla offered her 1873 Chart of the Solar System and a 1664 Map of the World poster that hung on her bedroom wall at the cottage. She said she would also mend the broken dolls' house in the attic that had once belonged to Storm's sister,

Maggie. 'That should make us a few bucks too!'

Tim promised to donate his stamp collection and a couple of autographed football shirts, but definitely *not* the model railway. Nor the telescope, he insisted. They had to stay in the family forever.

'And don't you dare get rid of my autograph book either,' Amelie said, glaring at her brother.

'As if,' Tim winked. 'Don't worry! Your secret is safe with me.' The autograph book with its precious cargo of signatures that included Mickey Mouse and Robbie Williams, (somehow acquired for their mum) had been his price for keeping silent about her unusual middle name. It was so easy to wind her up.

They set a date and time for the Sale and the playhouse meeting was officially brought to a close with plans to return in a week's time.

'You go write your amazing stories, Amelie,' said Isla, 'and we'll come up with a beautiful poster for your Grand Ballroom Sale.'

Chapter Sixteen
An Unexpected Discovery

For three days Tim and Isla scoured the Ballroom for suitable treasures, and odd places like the basement scullery and the little turret rooms upstairs. Storm filled a dozen cardboard boxes with old books, mostly blue and claret tomes, edged with gold. 'However, I'm never parting with these,' he said, pressing Volume One of Arthur Mee's *Children's Encyclopaedias* against his chest. 'These were my boy Ted's...' His voice cracked a little and Isla rushed forward to hug him.

Tim was given special permission to retrieve the broken dolls' house from the attic, and while he was there he hauled out the little mahogany table and the old oak cupboard with the damaged padlock. 'We'll clean these up in no time at all,' he said.

Towards the end of the week, Amelie joined them in the Ballroom. 'I need a break. My wrist aches from so much writing.'

'I'll type them up when you've finished,' Isla offered, thinking they might benefit from a little help with the spelling. 'It'll help me learn your funny British spellings,' she added tactfully. 'Colour, not color and so on.'

Amelie showed her gratitude by crawling into the walk-in wardrobe and hauling out the rest of the clothes. But just as she was heaving out the box of shoes, she got tangled up in a pile of wire coat hangers and fell sideways, crashing into the wooden panel at the back.

'Cheers, Amelie,' Tim groaned. 'Look, you idiot, you've broken it! You're so clumsy, we were doing just fine till you came in.'

But Amelie was far too interested in what was behind the broken wooden panel to take offence. She reached in and pulled the panel clear to reveal a small package, wrapped in old newspapers and tied with string. 'Hey, look what I've found!'

Tim snatched it from her and began to untie the string.

'Careful with the newspaper, Tim,' Isla warned. 'It looks very old.'

'There's a date here: August 1939 - that'll be just before World War Two.'

Inside were bundles of letters and sepia photographs, all wrapped in blue ribbon, and a collection of little leather notebooks, embossed with gold letters.

'Aunt Eggy's diaries!' Tim looked at his sister in amazement. 'Amelie Trott – you're a star!'

Amelie beamed. 'It was meant to happen, wasn't it?'

'And have you seen the inscription?' said Isla. 'E.T.!'

'Eglantyne Trott - extra-terrestrial! Tim grabbed Amelie by the shoulders and shook her affectionately. 'Your being clumsy really has paid off this time!'

'Here...' Isla passed Amelie a small, faded photograph, 'Eglantyne as a young girl. She's very pretty, like you.'

'Me?' Amelie, who had never thought of herself as pretty before, studied the little sepia photograph. Young Eggy was really rather nice. Not at all the grumpy old witch they'd always imagined; stomping around with a stick, ready to beat them if they dared to step out of line. She wore a long, flowing scarf and an enormous straw hat, tilted to one side and spiked with feathers. Untidy curls framed her perfect face. She had a neat little nose, covered in freckles, a bit like her own, and although she wasn't actually smiling, her eyes were; as though she'd just seen something funny. 'She's very *fambloyant*, isn't she?'

'Flamboyant, yes,' Isla agreed.

They carried the little package down to the study where an incredulous Storm inspected it with his magnifying glass. 'Good Lord,' he said, shaking his head. 'We can't possibly part with all this; far too precious. And who on earth found it, anyway?'

'Amelie did,' Tim said proudly, 'at the back of the wardrobe.'

'Well done, my girl, top marks!'

Amelie (who had never had top marks in anything) smiled. 'She is rather beautiful, isn't she? Can I keep this?' she asked, reluctant to let go of the little dog-eared photograph.

'Your reward,' nodded Storm.

'Did she have children?'

'Oh yes, dozens, hundreds, in fact.'

'What!'

'Not her own, obviously; she never married though she had plenty of admirers, as you can imagine.' He gently dusted the little photograph with his pocket handkerchief. 'Instead, she devoted her life to children in need, and not just to the children but to their families too. She was what you might call a free spirit.'

'Can we all have a read?' Tim asked. 'There might be some clues to the tunnels.'

'I insist you do!' Storm chuckled, 'but after the Sale though. For now, you have more than enough to do.' He fished out his crystal and held it up to the light for Tim and Isla to see. 'Never doubt for a moment that you will succeed!'

By the end of the week they were ready to take their Grand Ballroom Sale poster to Stanley, the printer. Between them they had scraped together just enough money for one hundred and fifty flyers and six large posters to place all around the town.

Grand Ballroom Sale

At Hadleigh House, Cloud Hill, Havenbridge
Sunday 29th July
6.30-9.30 pm
Vintage clothing & bric-a-brac
Antique furniture, Oriental rugs & wall hangings
Antiquarian books
Paintings by local artist Lucy Elizabeth Trott
Signed copies of books by local author Amelie J. Trott
Lots of Great Bargains & Delicious Refreshments
All Welcome!

'I really don't think you should have put *All Welcome!*' Amelie said. 'Just saying…'

'Too late,' Tim laughed. 'You worry too much. We need as many people here as possible.'

Isla smiled. 'Local author, Amelie J. Trott! By the way, what does the J stand for?' But Amelie was busying herself with a bag of five pence pieces and pretended not to hear.

Stanley said he'd do an extra big poster for his window. 'I'll bring the missus too,' he added enthusiastically. 'She loves old stuff.'

Charlie took one for the bakery and promised to give out one flyer with every purchase. 'Refreshments on me,' he added. 'I'll bring enough for everyone.'

'Thanks, Charlie,' Amelie said. 'And in return I'll give you a signed copy of one of my books.'

Tim counted out fifty flyers and placed them on his counter. 'Hey, Charlie, do you know anyone who could take a look at our house? It's costing us too much to repair and we may have to sell up. That's why we're having the Sale.'

'Well, we can't have that, can we? Yes, I know just the right bloke. My mate Gordon – he'll sort you out. You don't want to get ripped off.'

Next they called at the newsagents where Mrs Patel greeted them warmly and bobbed her head from side to side with great enthusiasm (which they already knew was the Indian way of saying yes). 'Only ten pence for two weeks,' she said, her hands dancing to the sound of her own lovely, musical voice. She placed a large poster in the middle of the window where everyone would see it.

On the way back into town they visited the library and got permission to pin a flyer on the notice board, then moved on to the fishing tackle shop where Kenny Pratt said he'd be very happy to be their auctioneer. 'You'll make more money that way,' he explained. 'Nice mahogany table here!' he said, adopting his auctioneer's voice. 'Any advances on a thousand pounds? Going... going... gone! Sold to Mr Pettifer!'

They all laughed. Mr Pettifer had a reputation for being the meanest man in Havenbridge; even though he was sitting on a fortune, Kenny Pratt tutted.

They hurried on to the Vicarage next and spoke to Reverend Jolley who seemed to have recovered now from his strange encounter the other week; then to the Police Station to have a word with Sergeant Buggeley. It was so cool and dark in there that the heat was a shock when they stepped outside again. The pavements were scorching and the sun hot on their backs, and they all had a single thought on their minds. 'The Harbour Café,' said Amelie who still had a pocketful of five pence pieces left over from the printers. 'Ice-creams on me...'

'Havenbridge Post Office and then we're done,' Tim said, counting out another batch of flyers. 'We'll ask Mrs Duff if she'll take some for the counter.'

Outside they spotted The Man in Black, as everyone called him. He had arrived in Havenbridge some months ago but no one seemed to know exactly who he was. They were discussing him now inside the Post Office. One or two people said they had seen him in some boring television programme that no one could remember the name of, while flicking through the channels.

'Bit of an odd-ball, that one,' Mrs Duff muttered unkindly behind the counter. 'Dresses like an old tramp.'

'Well dodgy, if you ask me,' agreed Sam Bolt, the postman. The Man in Black's house was hidden behind a barricade of fir trees at the end of a very long drive and Sam Bolt was the only person to have ventured onto his property. He had personally scrutinised his mail for clues to his identity but had so far come up with no more than a name: L.S. Goodman.

'Goodman. Well, that remains to be seen,' Miss Sowerbutts remarked suspiciously. 'Comes and goes at all hours.' Miss Sowerbutts was the local Neighbourhood Watch organiser and was an authority on all the inhabitants of Havenbridge. She kept a detailed record of everyone's comings and goings. 'I've got my eye on him.'

'No need for CCTV in Havenbridge then,' Tim said, loudly enough for her to hear.

The Man in Black was still there when they came out, sticking stamps on a pile of envelopes. He looked up and smiled as Amelie handed him a flyer and asked if he could perhaps take a few more.

He was rather scruffy, it was true, but not smelly at all, as they'd imagined. In fact he smelt fresh and lemony like the expensive soap shop in Littlehaven. And he wasn't old either although it was hard to tell behind his beard. He had lovely, kind eyes and a deep, cultured voice; and was rather handsome too, Amelie decided. The sort of man she could imagine wanting to marry one day. Or maybe even her mother?

'This looks rather interesting,' The Man in Black said. 'Mind if I bring a few friends? I'll take a few to Bookland for you, shall I? I'm just heading that way myself.'

In the distance they noticed a familiar white van. 'Eli Dankstone,' Tim said, pulling a face. 'That's who came to inspect our roof, Isla. We saw him in Devil's Gulley. He's in league with the Bottomley-Slighs, despite what Mona says about not knowing him.'

Isla nodded. 'Enough said.'

At that very moment, Eli Dankstone climbed out of his van and walked into the Hearts of Oak pub.

'There's someone else in the van,' Isla murmured. 'I'm sure I recognise the back of his head.'

'It's Magnus!' Tim pulled them both aside. 'Let's get out of here before they see us.'

'What if Eli Dankstone turns up?' Amelie gasped. 'Or Maynard and Magnus? They'll ruin it.'

'We'll worry about that if it happens. Anyway,' Tim said, 'we're safe. The Slighs are in Corfu that week, I remember Mum saying. And what could Eli possibly do to spoil things?'

'He's capable of anything,' Amelie said, her imagination running wild.

Chapter Seventeen
All Work and No Play

It took some time to convince Lucy Trott that decluttering the house was a very good thing.

'But these are all bits and bobs we might need one day,' she protested, waving a brass toasting fork.

'Mum,' Tim laughed, 'we've already got one toasting fork and when did we last use that? No one needs two.'

'And these,' she said, picking up a pair of elbow-length evening gloves that smelled unpleasantly of moth balls. 'You never know, I might want to wear these one day.'

Amelie sneezed and put them firmly back on the pile labelled *Things to be Sold*. 'You don't need evening gloves either. For one thing you never go anywhere to wear them.'

'But I might.'

'Then we'll buy you a new pair one day.'

'My mom declutters all the time,' Isla explained. 'She throws out anything she hasn't worn for a year. Oftentimes she'll fill a suitcase. It definitely makes room for new things to come into your life.'

'Like money,' Tim said.

'Hmm, hardly enough to pay for this house though…'

'You wait, it'll be the answer to all our problems,' Amelie insisted. 'And even if it doesn't pay for quite everything, it's a start.' She searched around for something to reinforce her argument. 'Anyway, Storm thinks it's a great idea.'

'And there's all your beautiful paintings,' Isla said excitedly. 'We'll showcase your work like a proper exhibition; and Amelie's books too. Everyone will come, we've made sure of that.'

'Not everyone,' Amelie insisted. 'Just the people we like and their friends.'

'I've even got a reporter coming from The Gazette,' Tim said.

After a lot of persuading and bargaining, Lucy agreed.

'Let's shake on it then.' Tim thrust out his hand. 'But you're not allowed into the Ballroom until we've finished. It has to be a surprise.'

'You won't forget my book covers, will you, Mum?' Amelie said, producing an old dog-eared photograph of Storm as a cheeky-faced schoolboy. 'I've written five out of six stories already. The last one should be finished tomorrow. Isla's going to type them all up for me.'

Tim went off in search of more articles for the Sale. There was still so much to do before their big day. 'By the way,' he called over his shoulder, 'we've got Charlie's mate Gordon coming next Sunday to look at the house. Let's see what he comes up with, eh?'

#

'I insist you take some time off,' Storm said towards the end of the week. 'No arguments. Get off to the beach and enjoy your holiday. All work and no play make Jack a very dull boy indeed.'

Which somehow reminded Amelie of school and her stomach turned over; still no report! At least the Sale was taking her mind off things a bit. She had now completed the last of her stories and Isla, who had now successfully mended and repainted the old dolls' house, had begun to type them up, tactfully editing out the worst of the spelling mistakes but leaving a few in for entertainment value.

'These stories are awesome, Amelie!' she proclaimed. 'Real page-turners, Storm will be so proud.'

Meanwhile, in the Ballroom, Tim had organised everything into categories: clothes and accessories; toys, books, ornaments and household goods; and one called Miscellaneous that included anything they weren't quite sure about. 'Like my signed football shirts and stamp collection,' he explained.

'We need some big signs,' Isla observed. 'I could do a few on my laptop.'

'Cool,' said Amelie. 'And will you do me one for my book-signing?'

'But of course.'

'Amelie,' Tim said, pointing to a large table near the stage, 'there's your table over there. Mum's paintings are here, facing the door so people will see them as soon as they walk in.'

'Where's best for Charlie's refreshments?' Amelie said, searching around for an electric socket. 'He's lending us his urn so we can sell hot drinks. What about here, near the door?'

Isla surveyed the Ballroom. It was all getting filled up quite quickly. 'I think Kenny, our auctioneer, should have the stage. And why don't we use the wind-up gramophone and play some of those lovely old records in the background? It'll create a real party atmosphere.'

'Yay!' Amelie began to waltz the length of the room, embracing some imaginary partner. 'Just like your dream!'

'Yes,' laughed Isla. 'All we need now are those fifty dollar bills…'

#

On the day before the Grand Ballroom Sale Tim guided his mother, duly blind-folded, up the stairs to the Ballroom. 'No peeping till we tell you!'

Isla brought up the rear with Storm. 'You badly need an elevator, guys. It's such a climb for poor Storm.'

'I know,' Amelie said, 'but there's the old servants' lift in the pantry; we'll get it working again once we have the money.'

'Ready, Mum?' Tim began to untie her blindfold. 'You can look now.'

There was a short pause while she blinked and took in the spectacle before her.

'Oh, my goodness, you've done all this!' Her eyes glistened. There were her paintings, all hung perfectly and illuminated with spotlights salvaged from Storm's study. She gazed around the enormous room, trying to take it all in: tables laden with forgotten treasures retrieved from disused rooms, brightly coloured signs everywhere, and even Amelie's little paperback books – it all looked so professional. 'I just hope plenty of people come; you really have done an excellent job, all of you.'

'Quite remarkable,' Storm agreed, 'and especially those marvellous books, young Amelie!' He put his arm around her shoulder. 'I'd pick you up and swing you around the room if I could. Wouldn't think I worked as a trapeze artist once, would you, Isla? Just another *Strange but True* story in Amelie's collection. Anyway, you all deserve a jolly good break now…'

The three children exchanged glances and grinned.

'Well,' said Tim, 'we thought we might camp outside tonight. But I checked the tent in the basement and with all the damp in there it's gone a bit mouldy…'

'So,' Amelie wheedled, clutching her mother's arm, 'we wondered about the playhouse. Since we cleaned it up there's definitely room for the three of us; five even with Lara and Freddie.'

'Oh, it would be such fun!' Isla said. 'And Dad's promised I can stay if it's ok with you.'

'Please say yes!' they all chorused.

A merry peal of laughter answered them. 'How could I possibly say no after you've all been so grown up and responsible? Of course you can! In fact, I'll make us a special supper before you go off on your travels! Remember though, no chatting till the early hours – you've got a very big day tomorrow.'

Chapter Eighteen
The Face at the Window

They dined on homemade pizzas and chips, followed by strawberries and pancakes, dripping with syrup and scoops of ice-cream. And just when they felt they could manage no more a tray appeared with mugs of steaming hot chocolate, topped with marshmallows.

'We'll sure sleep well tonight,' Isla said, yawning already.

With great excitement and hushed whispers they carried their sleeping bags down to the playhouse. Tim had already lugged the table indoors and replaced it with an old camp-bed he'd found in one of the turret rooms. 'You two can share the sofa-bed and I'll sleep on this.'

'I'll go and fetch Lara's and Freddie's baskets then,' Amelie said, running back to the house.

Isla yawned and stretched lazily. 'It really has been worth all the effort, hasn't it, Tim?'

Tim smiled. 'I guess we'll only know that when people arrive and start to part with their cash.'

The three companions chatted till the moon rose high in the sky. It was a clear and balmy night and one by one they drifted off to sleep; Tim first, then Isla, and lastly Amelie who was so excited she believed she never would. She had only been asleep for an hour when something woke her abruptly. Freddie and Lara had already stirred and were sitting on the floor in a pool of moonlight.

She stifled a scream and clutched the little crystal inside her pyjama pocket. 'Tim!' She reached over to shake him. 'There's someone outside, peering in…'

Drowsily, Tim opened his eyes and squinted vaguely around him until his gaze rested upon an unfamiliar face, framed by the window. A boy with enormous eyes stared back at them.

Isla was awake now too. 'Who is he?' she whispered.

'It's Dorin!' Amelie whispered. 'The new kid from school…He told me I should write a book!' She stared at the boy in disbelief.

Tim got up and opened the door just enough to take a better look at the boy. He was, at a guess, a little older than himself though not quite as tall. He had well-developed arms though and large hands that were busily occupied with a small gadget he was carrying.

'I-hope-I-didn't-startle-you,' Dorin said in his funny mechanical voice, 'but-my-transonometer–has-broken.'

Tim and Isla looked at each other, bewildered. '*Your what?*'

'Transonometer. It-helps-me-to-communicate-with-you-as-you're-not-very-good-at-reading-my-mind…' He paused. 'Not-yet-anyway.'

Then he grinned (if it could be called a grin for his mouth was so tiny and neat). 'I-can-read-yours-perfectly-though.'

'Who are you anyway?' Tim demanded.

'Sorry-how-rude-of-me.' The stranger hovered in the doorway and held up his hand in a form of salute. 'As-Amelie-said-I'm-Dorin.' He saluted again and Isla, too shocked to find words, instinctively raised her hand in response.

'Thank-you.' He placed a hand on his heart and bowed. As he did so his voice suddenly changed and he sounded perfectly normal. 'I had orders to come. I flew in earlier but am a little late because I had trouble with...' He hesitated. 'My aircraft.'

'Flew in!' Tim frowned. 'Which airport? The nearest one is miles away.' Anyway, he thought dubiously, he looked far too young to fly a plane himself.

'I'm older than I look,' Dorin laughed, as though hearing Tim's thoughts. 'We mature rather more quickly on my planet.' His big eyes glowed. 'Though we stay young and good-looking forever...' At this point, he began to wheeze with amusement. 'I'm about eighty-five in Earth years.'

'No way!' said Tim.

'You mean, you're an alien!' Isla gasped, remembering the TV programme she'd seen about aliens taking over the Earth. 'In America people are being kidnapped and taken on UFOs, and have horrible operations performed on them...'

Amelie shrunk further into her sleeping bag.

'Oh, Isla, do I really look like someone who will do you harm?'

He knew her name! 'But how do we *know?*' she persisted.

'What makes you think I'm an alien anyway?' As he spoke, his big eyes glowed and a light appeared in the centre of his chest. 'We don't even have that word in our language. In yours it means strange and unfamiliar but where I live we're all brothers and sisters at heart. Therefore aliens don't exist for us.' The light in his chest grew bigger and brighter. 'Sorry.' He grinned again. 'I really shouldn't show off. It's just that life on Zalnea is very different from here on Luga. That's what we call your planet, by the way - *Luga*. And I'm what is known as an Earth Watcher.'

The three children stared at one another, open-mouthed. An Earth Watcher, of course!

'Come in,' Tim said at once, making room on his camp-bed for their visitor. If this was a dream, it was the best one he'd ever had. 'Ouch! What did you pinch me for?'

'This is no dream, I assure you!' Dorin grinned

116

mischievously. 'This is for real.' He touched the symbol emblazoned on his chest. 'Just like your visit to Bookland, Amelie. Mind-wandering is just another kind of reality, essential for authors, of course.' He gave her a knowing look. 'Well done with your books. And yes, you were right. Storm did get kind of lost in Space one time…'

'He never said! How cool is that!' Amelie giggled while Tim and Isla looked on, bemused. 'You're even wearing the same badge as the Commander; a pair of hands holding a globe!'

'Yes, the Commander is my superior officer or *Tuló*. It was he who sent me. It's a great honour to be trusted with this mission.'

'*Tuló!* Oh, I do wish Storm was here.'

'Don't disturb him now, Amelie, but when you do see him please give him my best. I was one of the Watchers who saved him during the war.' Suddenly, he made to leave. 'But now I need your help urgently. My craft is parked on Storm's runway.' He pointed in the direction of the fields behind the hangar. 'I have to move it before sunrise.'

Guided by bright moonlight, the children followed him outside and made their way with him to the hangar.

'I've sent for assistance so with luck I'll take off and be gone before daybreak. If not, we'll have to move it somewhere a bit more secluded.'

He led them to a large dome-shaped craft stationed behind the hangar, in full view of the fields and glinting in the moonlight. There were small portholes and rows of lights all around the lower edge.

'It's quite small as space-crafts go. My co-pilot was sent on another mission so I had to come alone.'

'It's a lot bigger than Storm's microlight,' Tim said.

'This is a Scoutship, Tim. Motherships can be as big as houses, others the size of small towns. Remember those "lanterns" you saw recently? This was one of them.' Dorin stooped to stroke Freddie and pat Lara's head. 'And it was you two clever creatures who spotted us first.'

He tapped on the side of the craft and immediately an opening appeared. 'Anyway, let's see if we can get this going… Hop in!'

'No way am I going up in that!' Amelie said firmly. 'Never!'

Dorin smiled. 'Why ever not? It's perfectly safe.'

Amelie still looked dubious. 'Can Lara and Freddie come too?'

'But of course. Come and see…'

Inside was a small, softly lit hallway which led into a control room. Here there were low, padded seats and, directly above them, a very bright circular light.

'Sit down,' Dorin instructed. The far wall was completely covered with dials and coloured lights and strange symbols. He positioned himself before them and at once the lights began to change colour, blinking on and off in rapid succession.

'That's a relief.' The bright central light began to whir and he turned to give them a thumbs-up. 'It's been fixed remotely; looks like everything's in good working order now. We have lift off, my friends!'

The three children braced themselves for a jolt but a minute or two passed and still nothing seemed to have happened.

'What's up?' Isla asked, waiting for the familiar roar of a rocket launch or an aeroplane take-off. 'Engine failure?'

Dorin laughed. 'Not at all, Isla. We're flying right over Germany now. Just a short trip around Luga this time. Next time we'll go further, maybe to your Moon; or even to my home planet, Zalnea.'

'But why no sound of an engine?'

'Because we have mastered gravity, Isla. We use the elements to sail on the waves of space; like a ship on the

Cosmic Ocean. Look…' He pointed to a giant television screen right above them. 'We are already over the Ural Mountains…'

'Somewhere between Europe and Russia then,' said Tim. 'But that's like thousands of miles away and it's taken no more than two minutes!'

'What!' Isla gasped. 'How can that possibly work? I've always wanted to be an airline pilot but I think I've changed my mind. Yes,' she laughed, 'I'll be the first female astronaut to land on – where did you say, Dorin - Zalnea?'

'Oh, yes! You'll learn to do all this in time, Isla. But as yet your Earth is far from ready. To reveal the secrets of gravity to your scientists would be extremely dangerous. Were they to find their way into the hands of certain evil men and women on your planet…' he paused, leaving them to ponder on the possible consequences… 'Our Solar System, our Galaxy; indeed, the Cosmos itself would be in grave danger.'

'So what can we do?' Amelie asked.

'It's quite simple actually. Once you Lugans learn to see one another as yourselves will you cease to do harm, and then all the wonders of creation will be revealed to you!'

Amelie shivered with excitement, remembering her recent conversation with Storm. 'We really aren't alone in the universe, are we?'

'Absolutely not, Amelie; life exists everywhere.'

She peered intently through one of the portholes. 'Where are we now then?'

'Just over the Himalayas. Look…' Dorin indicated the giant screen once more. 'There's Mount Everest, Tim.'

'But we've been flying for no time at all.'

'Exactly.' Dorin smiled. '*No time at all*. See, there's China… Shall we send out a couple of photographic probes?'

They watched as two balls of light appeared on the screen, heading for Earth.

'We like to take photos of your planet whenever we can.

It helps us with our understanding of Luga. They also make rather nice pictures for our walls. Luga is one of the wonders of the Cosmos, some say the most beautiful.'

'Those probes must be what chased the vicar and Sergeant Buggeley,' Amelie said, remembering her chat with Charlie.

Dorin grinned. 'Gave them quite a shock, I expect. Their pictures are now in our Gallery of Life on Luga. A policeman and a vicar – such things we don't have on Zalnea.' The lights on the control panel danced wildly and changed colour once more. 'Now then, my friends, we'd better move on and get you back home. You have a momentous day ahead of you.'

Amelie gasped: 'Our Ballroom Sale! With all this happening I'd completely forgotten.'

'Anyone you'd care to visit on our way back?'

'Yes please!' There was only one person Isla longed to see. 'My mom if we can...'

The big screen went blurred and soon a small apartment block came into view.

'Hey, we're in Georgetown!' Isla cried, unable to contain herself. 'That's exactly where we live.' She shook her head in amazement. A chance meeting with two strangers on a beach, and now this! No one would believe her, of course, which was exactly what Tim and Amelie were thinking too. Not that they cared. *They* knew it was true and that was all that mattered.

'Nice place!' Tim said. 'Somehow I'd expected a big city with bright lights and loads of cars. This looks all green and peaceful.'

'It is,' Isla said, 'though still not too far from the city.'

'Look, Isla, there's your mom.' Dorin adjusted the view and zoomed in further. 'Preparing dinner, by the look of it; it's still Saturday evening here.'

Isla's voice was choked with tears. 'Will she know I can see her…?'

No sooner had she spoken than Isla's mother became

bathed in a soft golden light.

'I think that's your answer,' Dorin said gently. 'See, she's turning to look at something now; a display of photographs on the wall.'

'They're pictures of me, taken just before I left for England!'

'That's so cool! I'd love to see where The Man in Black lives,' Amelie said. 'Is that a bit nosy, do you think? His real name is Mr Goodman; he's such a lovely man but everyone calls him a tramp.'

Dorin smiled. 'Ah, but that's because they don't know him like we do. I'm sure he'd be delighted to have you visit.'

'You mean you know Mr Goodman?'

Once again the screen went fuzzy and gradually a number of tall, dark trees appeared and behind them a very long drive. Dorin moved in closer to show them an elegant white house, covered in ivy and climbing roses; then closer still until they were looking directly into a small study. There was Mr Goodman seated at his desk, hunched over a pile of books.

'What a warm heart he has!' Dorin observed. 'A very Good Man indeed.'

Once again, a soft golden light flooded the room. It held Mr Goodman in a bright bubble as he bent down to pick up a sheet of paper that had fallen to the floor.

Tim gaped. 'That's our Ballroom flyer!'

I hope you don't spy on us, Amelie thought, remembering how untidy her bedroom was. I wouldn't like anyone looking in through my window.

'Of course not!' Dorin laughed, and Tim and Isla both wondered why that was since no one had actually spoken. 'We watch over you, yes, but we never invade your privacy.'

They all looked at one another in amazement. He really did know everything about them but in the nicest possible way.

They had already landed safely on Storm's little runway. The invisible doorway opened up once more and soon they found themselves standing at the back of the hangar. Everything was so quiet and still it might never have happened. Tim glanced at his phone. They had stepped aboard the Scoutship only moments ago and had already travelled the globe.

They were all thinking exactly the same thing. First the ten foot tall man and now an elderly man (who looked no more than a boy) who had just flown in from a planet called Zalnea! Yet somehow, in a strange kind of way, it all seemed perfectly normal.

'Thank you, Dorin!' they chorused. It had been, they agreed, the most incredible trip of their lives.

'But there's more still to come,' Dorin promised, his big eyes glowing. 'Now hurry back and get some sleep!' He raised his right arm in salute, touched his chest, and bowed deeply. 'Goodbye, Lara. Goodbye, little Freddie! I shall see you all again very soon.'

Silently, they made their way back to the playhouse and soon fell into a deep and dreamless sleep.

They awoke many hours later to the sound of Storm banging on the window with his stick. 'It's gone eleven,' he bellowed. 'Rise and shine - it's your Big Day!'

Chapter Nineteen

The Grand Ballroon Sale

Tim yawned, swung his legs off the camp bed and slipped his feet into his trainers. 'Okay, okay, I'm coming.' Sunlight streamed into the little playhouse and he shaded his eyes. 'It can't be that late, surely…'

'Too much gassing and not enough sleep…' barked Storm and squatted on the end of the camp bed. 'You heard what your mother said. No chatting till the early hours!'

'Don't blame us,' Tim said gruffly. 'We had a visitor, an old friend of yours.'

'Visitor? Friend of mine? At night, for heaven's sake?'

'Little guy, very young looking for his age,' Isla giggled. 'He sends his regards.'

'What?' Storm looked completely baffled. 'You've lost me, I'm afraid…'

'Dorin, of course!' Amelie laughed.

'Dorin? You mean my old friend's been here and you didn't bother to fetch me? I haven't seen him since, well…'

They all knew he meant That Terrible Day. 'Because he told us we mustn't disturb you,' Amelie said gently. 'Don't worry, he promised he'd be back.'

They all talked over one another, desperate to share their stories: how they'd hovered over the Himalayas, sent little probes out over China; even zoomed down to Isla's apartment in Georgetown, Washington.

'The Earth Watchers' technology is remarkable,' Storm mused, 'but what they've really come to teach us is how to live.'

'Yes,' Isla said, still unable to take it all in. 'I got that impression already. The world looks a very small place from a spacecraft…'

Storm nodded, remembering his own first trip in a Scoutship. 'You're very honoured, you know. Not many people get the chance…'

'But you did!' Tim said. 'And is it true you got lost in Space?'

Storm smiled. 'Yes, just another "Strange but True" story, which our Amelie has picked up on for her book.'

At that moment they heard Charlie's friend Gordon arrive so they all trooped off to join him, and sat, bleary-eyed, in the kitchen while Lucy poured mugs of tea.

'A bit late for breakfast, you lot,' she laughed and gave them all a big chunk of fruit cake instead. 'Mrs Chumbley just brought it in with the eggs. Gordon, you must have some too.'

They chatted about the Sale for a while and Gordon said he was looking for something a bit special for the wife's birthday.

'Does she like reading?' Amelie asked casually.

'Well yes, as a matter of fact, she does. I was thinking of a bookcase if you have one.'

Amelie's face fell. 'Oh, well yes, we do have a big oak one. Perhaps you'd like one of my books for it?'

But Gordon was gulping down the last of his tea before hurrying off to inspect the roof and the attic. He returned a little later, voicing the firm opinion that someone had already been up there, *wreaking far more damage than any flaming storm.*

'No wonder your bloomin' attic's flooded. Someone's

made a flippin' great hole in the roof…!'

'And I wonder who that could be…!' Storm muttered.

'Nicked a load of lead too, not to mention felting and tiles…'

'Elias Dankstone!' Lucy's hand flew to her mouth.

Amelie sighed. 'I told you I saw him creeping around weeks ago, and then those tiles in the back of his van!'

Gordon shook his head. Why would Dankstone want to do that, he wondered? Everyone knew how hard-up the Trotts were; barely two pennies to rub together since That Terrible Day…

'You must have heard of the Stones,' Storm said, 'and our underground tunnels.'

'Old wives' tales, I've always thought. Bad bunch though, those Dankstones, always have been.'

Storm nodded and crossed his fingers. 'Like that with the Slighs, it appears. Thick as thieves the lot of them.'

'Thick, yes… and thieves right enough!' Gordon snorted. 'And as for his estimate, Mrs Trott, chuck it in the bin! We'll have this lot sorted for you in no time at all.'

'Oh, Gordon…' she began. 'I don't know how to thank you.'

'It's a pleasure, Mrs Trott. You're good folks, all of you. Nicest kids I know.' He nodded at Tim, Amelie and Isla and held out his plate for another slice of cake. 'You must be very proud of your little family.'

'I am,' she replied, not bothering to point out that Isla wasn't actually a Trott, since they now all thought of her as one.

Gordon packed up his things and waved them all a cheery goodbye. 'See you tonight, then!' He winked at Amelie. 'And put me down for one of them books.'

They watched as his old van disappeared down the drive.

'What a sweet man,' Lucy said with a big sigh of relief. She gathered up a bundle of brightly coloured flags from the kitchen table. 'Look what I found earlier. Come on, everyone – time we put the flags out! Let's show the world that we Trotts won't be defeated!'

Later, she went off to tidy the dining room just in case anyone visiting the Grand Ballroom Sale might come downstairs and see what a dreadful mess they all lived in. Having organised a number of unpaid bills into one big pile she eventually came upon an unopened letter in a handwritten envelope. She tore it open and pulled out two carefully folded sheets. Her heart sank. She scanned the accompanying letter to the end... *and I must therefore ask you to make alternative arrangements for your daughter for the coming year.* Signed: Ernestine Snarkey.

Amelie expelled - and the only other school was over ten miles away! Angrily, she tossed the letter aside. She would deal with that later.

Kenny Pratt was the first to arrive that evening, looking very dapper in a tweed jacket and colourful bow tie. He had brought with him a microphone and a pair of large speakers.

'Testing, testing!' he boomed. 'One-two, one-two... Everything to be auctioned except for the paintings and books, right, guys?'

'Yep!' said Tim. 'We've arranged all the chairs in rows for the auction.'

Isla was helping Charlie to set up a little café near the door. There were cakes and sandwiches on sale, and plenty of coffee and tea, as well as Storm's homemade lemonade. Sam Bolt, the postman, had even thought to bring some bottles of homemade hedgerow wine for the adults.

Amelie was eyeing her book display. Not exactly Bookland but it was a start, at least. Mum had done a great job with the covers and handsome young Storm looked the perfect hero. Her main concern now was the book signing.

She had settled on a signature that wouldn't take too long. 'Keep it simple,' Isla had suggested. 'You'll be signing so many you won't have time for loops and curls.'

A.J. Trott already sounded like a successful author's name. But then to confuse things everyone kept saying what a nice name Amelie was and how the J made it more professional, so *Amelie J. Trott* it became once more.

'What is the *J* anyway?' Isla asked one more time but at that very moment a girl and a boy walked in. Both wore large horn-rimmed spectacles and were dressed primly in identical blazers with white shirts and sharply pressed trousers. Miss Snarkey's Special Agents had arrived with notebooks in hand. They snooped around for a while then sat down, blank-faced, in one corner, watching and murmuring occasionally out of the corner of their mouths without turning their heads.

'Weirdos,' said Tim.

'Snarkey's spies, Isla,' Amelie hissed. 'Jonathan and Felicity Speck.'

Isla laughed. 'They look harmless enough.'

'But they're not. Don't tell them a thing.'

Isla nodded and pretended to draw a zip across her mouth.

The next to turn up were Dr Batty and his sister Georgina. They headed straight for the paintings and chose two colourful landscapes for Cloud Cottage. Amelie watched with interest. Dr Batty had entered into a lively conversation with her mother and was showing her some photographs of Isla.

'Do you think you could paint her in time for Christmas?' he whispered. 'She mustn't know, of course; it has to be a complete surprise.' They both laughed and Lucy winked conspiratorially, implying his secret would be safe with her.

Tim happened to look up at that very moment and caught Amelie's impish smile.

'What are you up to, Amelie Trott?'

'Nothing; why?'

'I don't believe you. You've got that look on your face.'
He gave her a warning nod, as if to say *don't go there*.

'If you must know, I was thinking about decluttering and
how it brings new things into your life. Maybe that includes
new people too.' It was time their mother met someone nice,
and if that someone was Dr Andrew Batty then Isla would
end up as their sister; how cool would that be!

'Amelie, no!'

Amelie shrugged and wandered back to her bookstand.
The big clock on the wall showed it was now two minutes to
seven and only a handful of people had so far arrived.

'Supposing nobody comes,' she fretted. All our hard work
– and for nothing...' She began to pace the floor forlornly.
Even her little crystal did little to reassure her.

'They will,' Tim said, stretching out on an old sofa,
labelled "Not for Sale." 'Just trust!'

'Yes, let's put some music on to cheer you up,' Isla said,
winding up the old gramophone. 'Even if we don't sell
everything, we'll still have had a lovely evening.'

But Amelie refused to be pacified. 'No, we won't. It'll be
awful.' The wretched Voice of Doubt was intent on causing
a scene. She turned to glare at the Secret Agents as though it
must somehow be their fault.

A man with a big camera walked in. He peered around
the room for a while then frowned and headed for the door
once more. Seeing him, Tim leapt to his feet. 'It's the reporter
from the Gazette! Hey, Kevin, come back!'

But soon he returned with Kevin in tow. 'Storm's selling
raffle tickets at the door,' he explained, finding Kevin a
chair. 'That's what's been holding up the queue. I knew it
was nothing to worry about. What a great turn out!'

'Yes, look out the window,' Isla called. 'There's a massive
queue down there!'

Very soon footsteps echoed up the stairs and a great flood
of visitors swept into the Ballroom.

Chapter Twenty
A Surprising Offer

The first was Mr Goodman. He appeared to be very interested in Lucy Trott's paintings too, especially what he called her *hyper-realistic* portraits.

'Lawrence Goodman,' he announced, shaking her hand. 'I have one or two contacts in London, gallery owners. Unfortunately, they'll be a little late as their train was delayed. I do hope you haven't sold out completely by then. I know they'll be most impressed.'

He moved on to tour the room, stopping here and there to view the antiquarian books and wall hangings, and making notes as he went. Finally, he came to Amelie's bookstand and picked up twelve copies.

'I'd like all of these signed, please,' he said. 'Then, should you get famous someday, I'll make a fortune from these lovely original copies.' He handed a wad of bank notes to Isla who was in charge of the till (an old plastic toy till she had moved to the "Not for Sale" items), and with that he went off to await the auction.

When Isla unfurled the bank notes and saw how much Mr Goodman had left she let out a squeal of surprise. 'Wow, two hundred and forty pounds! That's twenty pounds a copy, Amelie!'

Amelie's face flushed with pleasure. 'I must save one for

Charlie's wife. Which do you think she'd like?'

'Let's see…' Isla thought carefully. 'I think she'd like a romantic story best. I saw her reading a Mills and Boon on the beach.'

'Sloppy love stories?' Amelie pulled a face. 'No, I'm sure Storm never had time for any of that. He was too busy having adventures.'

'What about the one where he meets Louisa during the war? That's kind of cute… You should have called it *Love is in the Air* or something…'

The Special Agents busily noted everything down but were soon interrupted by Tim who asked them if they'd like a cake and something to drink. 'All in a good cause,' he forced himself to say cheerily and was rewarded at once with a dual eye-roll that seemed to suggest: 'You call *this* a good cause?'

Storm had now left his post at the door with Gordon in charge of the raffle and any stray guests. 'Oh, my giddy aunt!' he cried, hearing music playing on the old gramophone. He had some very strange sayings. 'I haven't heard this one for a while – Jack Hylton and 'Happy Days Are Here Again'!' He glanced around the room and spotted the Neighbourhood Watch person eyeing the auction display.

'Fancy a dance, Miss Sowerbutts?' he said, attempting a bow and almost falling over. 'I see you have a very nice pair of velvet evening gloves there. You'll be the belle of the ball!'

Miss Sowerbutts (who had only come to inspect the inside of the house which she'd heard from old Mrs Duff was dreadfully untidy and in need of a proper clean), went very red. She explained she'd got a bad knee, and anyway the gloves were for her sister, adding that she herself had never danced in her life and wasn't about to start now, thank you very much.

Overhearing this, plump Mrs Chumbley from the farm (already a bit tipsy on hedgerow wine) jumped to her feet and said she'd be only too happy. She then proceeded to drag a bemused Storm around the floor in an energetic quickstep, warbling 'Happy Days are here again...,' at the top of her voice... 'Your cares and troubles are gone...'

The reporter from the Gazette took a number of fine action shots of Mrs Chumbley's curious dance routine. 'Front page!' He grinned and helped himself to another glass of hedgerow wine.

'On the house, Kevin,' Charlie said, hoping to get a mention in the Gazette. Charlie's cakes were selling like – well, hot cakes, he quipped; and since all the sandwiches had gone already Tim had to run downstairs to make some more.

Once the room was full and all the seats were occupied Kenny, the auctioneer, began. 'First lot coming up...' he announced, and everyone grew quiet.

Sergeant Buggeley bought a collection of crime novels, and the vicar, Reverend Jolley, secured a set of antiquarian books and a football shirt for his nephew. Gossipy Mrs Duff was persuaded to bid for a small oriental rug, which she did, grudgingly, having first inspected it for stains and discounted any unpleasant smells, on account of them keeping two animals in the house which she considered dreadfully unhygienic. She would, she declared, give it a good going over in the yard with some carpet shampoo before it entered the house.

Sam Bolt bagged Tim's collection of postage stamps dating back to the 1930s, and Gina from the Chippy bought the two porcelain dolls with real hair for her twin girls.

Miss Sowerbutts not only claimed the velvet gloves but also splashed out on a pair of WW2 binoculars for her neighbourhood watching. Mrs Patel found an ornamental Indian fan that reminded her of home, and Stanley the printer succeeded in out-bidding a local antiques dealer for Maggie's newly renovated dolls' house. Gordon purchased not only the oak bookcase but also the mahogany table, brass toasting fork, and a stuffed bird in a cage; plus a signed copy of *Wild Billy Storm's Adventures in Outer Space* for his wife.

Mr Pettifer, the meanest man in Havenbridge, purchased a china teacup and then went back to the café for more cake and sandwiches without paying.

Then Kenny mistakenly announced the last lot as the "Not for Sale" sofa which no one had the heart to mention since it finally went for £265, thanks to Mr Goodman's generous last bid.

Eventually his gallery friends arrived and caused much excitement by unhesitatingly offering Lucy an exhibition in London.

'Does that mean Mum will be famous?' Amelie asked Mr Goodman.

'With your mother's great talent, I rather think so,' he replied. 'She'll get lots of commissions as a result. By the way, speaking of talent, I like your books very much, Amelie. I read them while the auction was in progress. I hope you'll continue to write such interesting and hilarious stories.' He especially loved *Up to His Tricks: Wild Billy Storm's Book of Practical Jokes*; and the circus story where he worked as a trapeze artist, bounced off the fat man's belly and ended up being caught in the elephant's trunk. 'But this is my personal favourite, from *Billy Storm and His Snail Sanctuary*:

Billy Storm had a very fine garden, resplendent with exotic flowers and vegetables. However, he also adored snails, nemesys (arch enemys) of gardeners the world over. Evrytime he trod on a snail he would apologise sincerely and give it a proper funeral in his garden. 'Snail dust to dust, snail ashes to ashes, gone but not forgotten, RIP, and I promise never to tred on anything living again. Amen.' Of course, this made walking on pavements rather compilcated so one day he decided instaed to travel by microlight aircraft. This was, of course, a good deal safer as long as you didn't bump into birds…'

'Marvellous!' He laughed till tears spilled onto his cheeks.

Amelie looked at him quizzically. 'But it's not meant to be funny,' she retorted. 'And it's all absolutely true…'

'Ah, but then you're a very modest young lady who doesn't quite realise her talent for entertaining others. You have a real gift.'

'I'm glad you like them. They're about my Great-Grandpa Trott.'

'And your mother designed the covers, eh? Quite beautiful! What do you say if we gather all your stories into one novel and I give you an advance?'

Amelie's eyes widened with curiosity.

'It's a payment for books you haven't yet written. I run a publishing company in London. I'll need to discuss this with your mother and old Mr Trott, of course, but I'm thinking of five thousand for this one…'

Amelie hesitated, unable to believe her ears. 'Hey, did you really mean *pounds*?'

'What else?' He grinned. 'And another five thousand for the next…'

Ten thousand pounds for doing what she loved most? Amelie considered for a moment then nodded. 'I'd like that very much, Mr Goodman…'

Tim and Isla had already emptied the till and were adding up everything they'd sold. With the auction and Lucy's paintings, then Amelie's books, plus the raffle and Charlie's café, it all amounted to the grand sum of six thousand, eight hundred and seventy-seven pounds and fifty-three pence. The three pence, they decided, was Mr Pettifer's contribution for two enormous platefuls of cake and sandwiches and several cups of tea. Now, thanks to Gordon, and with Mr Goodman's advance, they would have more than enough to save the house and pay all the bills.

Amelie thought of all the extra things she'd planned to buy: new carpets; a china dinner service and a pair of evening gloves for her mother; as well as a lift (Isla called it an elevator) for Storm…

'Thank you, Mr Goodman,' she sang, and rushed forward to hug him. 'Dorin really was right about you!' It slipped out before she could stop herself.

'Dorin?'

'Oh, just a friend of ours,' Amelie said, her cheeks burning a little.

'I will, as I said, have to consult with your mother. Get her approval.'

Amelie smiled. 'Mum will be very, very happy, Mr Goodman.'

He reached out his hand. 'Shall we shake on it then? And do call me Lawrence.'

The Specks watched closely as Amelie took his hand. Their Special Assignment hadn't been quite what they'd hoped for and, dejected, they closed their notebooks and prepared to report back to headquarters. 'Perhaps,' said Felicity Speck sideways, 'we'll tell her the whole thing was a flop.'

Jonathan Speck nodded. 'Don't mention the publisher. Just say a lot of people were drunk and disorderly and the police had to be called.' He jerked his head towards Sergeant Buggeley. 'She'll like that a lot.'

'And we'll remind her about that protest march too,' Felicity Speck said slyly.

Amelie rushed over to share her good news with Tim and Isla, and Kenny and Charlie. She glanced back at her new friend Lawrence, and waved. He was really rather good-looking. Perhaps he and her mum…? Already a story was forming in her mind but she had to stop right there because she had spotted someone coming in through the door.

Eli Dankstone looked about him. Ignoring the NO

SMOKING signs Isla had made, he lit up a cigarette, then sidled over to Kenny Pratt who was clearing up his auctioneer's table.

'Successful Sale then?' he jeered, picking up a tatty old cushion and a broken stool. Next he spotted an old mask that someone had dropped on the floor, kicked it across the room then changed his mind and stuffed it inside his jacket.

'Champion!' Kenny replied with a satisfied sigh. 'At least they won't need to sell up anymore.' The Sale was something he'd felt personally responsible for and everyone had given him a huge cheer at the end.

Eli Dankstone's face darkened. He'd only come to gloat. 'You're kidding me! Selling a few manky bits of furniture?'

Kenny shook his head. 'The girl's only got herself a publishing deal! Who'd have thought it, at ten years old?'

Eli drew hard on his cigarette. 'Nah, this place is falling apart.'

Kenny folded his arms across his chest. 'They've got old Gordon to sort it though. Someone who won't rip them off,' he added pointedly. He'd never thought much of Elias Dankstone, always cheating at cards in the pub.

Suddenly overwhelmed by all their good news, Amelie gazed out of the Ballroom window. The little flags that lined the drive were waving merrily in the evening breeze. Not even Eli Dankstone could disturb her anymore. She remembered how anxious she'd been earlier in case no one turned up. How quickly things could change! And as though to prove this an unbidden thought entered her mind: her missing report. No, she resolved, she would worry about that later. At least the house was now safe and Eli Dankstone and the Bottomley-Slighs were no longer a threat.

There were still a few people hovering about, chatting and saying goodbye. 'Best party I've been to in years,' she heard tipsy Mrs Chumbley say.

Amelie turned and watched Tim and Isla clearing up the

mess; Isla was sweeping the floor and Tim busily collecting rubbish in a black bin liner.

'Nothing to worry about now,' he said contentedly. 'Mum was right, us Trotts won't be beaten, and that includes you, Isla.'

Isla gave him one of her startlingly beautiful smiles.

'I'll be back in a moment,' Amelie said. 'Just something I have to do.' Ignoring Eli Dankstone, she closed the door behind her and walked unhurriedly downstairs, savouring the sense of relief, and unable to quite believe how well things had finally turned out. Together they had saved Hadleigh House – and she was soon to become a published author!

She paused at her favourite place and sat, cradling her knees. Late sunlight shone through the moons and stars in Aunt Eggy's stained glass window, scattering rainbows on the stairs. She looked around to make sure she was still alone then took out the little crystal from her pocket and held it up to the light. It was more beautiful than ever. She gazed up at the window once more. But of course! How had she not seen it before? That was where he had disappeared, the ten foot tall man. Light radiated from the figure with the outstretched hand… Of course, it was Dorin's *Tuló* – the Commander!

Eli Dankstone tossed his cigarette on the floor and stubbed it out with the toe of his boot. This calls for a change of plan, he thought sourly, and left the room to call Maynard who was holidaying in Corfu. No answer. He tapped his foot impatiently; he'd forgotten they were two hours ahead over there. He waited while someone passed him on the stairs then, in a low voice, left a voicemail instead:

'Maynard, we need to act fast, mate; find that Stone, get access to the tunnels. Otherwise, Mr Sligh, we'll resort to Plan B and grab the old man.' He laughed maliciously. 'And I'm sure your lad will be only too happy to help…'

Several days passed and a pleasant hush fell over Hadleigh House. The warm weather continued and everyone agreed that they hadn't seen such a summer for years. Old Storm pottered happily in his vegetable garden while Lucy, happy for the first time in years, began a series of commissions for the gallery owners in London.

Despite her fears, Amelie had become very curious about her missing report. Weeks had now passed yet still it hadn't appeared. Perhaps now would be a good time to mention it; get it out of the way before the end of the holidays. She went off in search of her mother and found her upstairs, sorting out her wardrobe.

'Decluttering, Mum?'

'I thought I'd take Isla's advice,' Lucy said, heaving a pile of clothes onto her bed. 'I'll never wear these again...'

Amelie picked up an old woollen jumper and hugged it to her like a little stuffed toy. 'I've got something to ask you...'

'Fire away then.' Lucy closed the wardrobe doors. 'There, all done. Pass me that bin liner, will you?'

'It's about my report...'

'Ah, that.'

'I was wondering – you see, Snarkey said she'd post

it because it was so *astroshus* and Tim never gave you his because of course it's brilliant as usual and he didn't want to show me up which was kind of ...'

'Hey, slow down, girl!' Lucy had a strange smile on her face. 'Atrocious maybe but I think it's time I had harsh words with Ernestine Snarkey...'

'You mean you've had it all this time?' Amelie covered her mouth and giggled. 'And is that *really* her name?'

Lucy threw back her head and laughed too. 'Yes, I found it the day of the Sale and tossed it straight in the bin. I'm seriously considering an official complaint...'

'But you never said...'

'Come here, my angel!' She reached out her arms and hugged Amelie to her. 'What you've achieved recently is worth far more than any silly old report. Your wonderful imagination has not only saved Hadleigh House but made an author of you too!' She kissed the top of her head. 'Amelie, everyone is special in their own way, something Miss Snarkey seems to have overlooked. And you can tell Tim I'm proud of him too, not just for having another brilliant report but for being such a kind and loyal brother.'

#

The children spent the next few days on the beach, aware that all too soon Isla would be returning to Washington for the start of the new school year.

'Time's going too fast,' Amelie said. 'We must do something extra special before you go.'

'But it's all been special, every single moment,' said Isla.

'Mmm...' Tim consulted his collection of maps. 'Let's find somewhere we've never been before.'

Isla smiled wistfully. 'I hope I get to see Dorin again.'

The next few days passed quietly. Isla's father had at last managed to take some time off, and Amelie, with a bit of help from Storm's old diary, set to work on *More Extraordinary*

Adventures of Wild Billy Storm.

'Here, I've made a list of useful words. What do you think, Tim?'

Iniment = very soon
Resorsfull = clever
Onimus = very scary
Nofairyus = evil

'Mmm, very good,' Tim said tactfully, 'though you might want to change the spellings a bit?'

Amelie shook her head. 'Lawrence likes them, no idea why. I'm always in trouble for getting spellings wrong at school. You just never know with adults, do you?'

Tim hoped she'd be allowed back to Havenbridge next term and wouldn't have to travel all the way to Littlehaven. 'Yeah,' he agreed, 'they can be rather unpredictable.' With that he returned to his model railway which had grown considerably and now took up most of the sitting room. 'I'll have to have to find somewhere bigger for this,' he sighed. 'Once the attic's repaired, I'll take it up there.' He rummaged around in the chest for the little tin of World War 2 Aircraft and Airmen. Yes, there it was, right at the bottom. He prised it open and tipped out its contents: model fighter planes, all built to scale, and dozens of tiny hand-painted figures. But two in particular took caught his eye.

'Hey, look at this.' He handed his sister the smaller of the two figures.

'Wow, that's Dorin!' She picked up the larger figure and examined it carefully. 'And this one's the Commander... How did they get in there?'

'Do you think Storm made them?'

Intrigued, they went off in search of Storm and finally found him standing in the kitchen doorway, shaking earth off his trowel. 'Just look at the size of these cabbages!' he said proudly, holding one aloft.

'You'll win first prize in the Havenbridge Show with that,'

Tim said. 'You joining us, Storm?' The old man murmured gratefully and Tim filled the kettle and arranged three mugs on a tray.

Amelie stared in awe at the enormous cabbage. 'How did that happen?'

'We had a bumper crop like this in 1939, just before the start of the war,' he reminisced. 'Giant potatoes and tomatoes as big as pumpkins… Eggy said it was all down to the Earth Watchers.'

'Pity everyone thought she was mad,' Amelie said, searching for a packet of chocolate biscuits. 'I believe anything's possible… especially since meeting the Commander and Dorin. Tim, show Storm what you found.'

'Good Lord, I've not seen these before,' Storm said, peering at the two little painted figures. He turned them over in his hand then took out his magnifying glass to inspect the label on the tin. 'This looks like your father's writing.' He scratched his head thoughtfully. 'Michael must have made them as a child. But how on earth he managed to capture their likeness is a mystery. Wait here a minute, you two…'

He shuffled off to his study and returned a little later with Aunt Eggy's diaries. 'Have a read of these, Tim. Amelie's got enough to do writing her latest book.'

Amelie pouted. 'But I want to read them too.'

'You will, we'll share them,' Tim said.

'I suppose.' Amelie yawned and began to gather up her things. 'I'm tired anyway. I want to be up with the lark tomorrow.'

Tim, who was already deeply engrossed in the diaries, glanced up vaguely and waved but Storm smiled and kissed the top of her head. 'Goodnight then, my dear! Sleep well.'

#

Eli Dankstone had spent the evening in the Hearts of Oak, brooding over his brown ale and pork scratchings. His mind was fixed on the tunnels. Rumour had it there was an entrance at the top of the fields near old Storm Trott's shed with another somewhere inside the house. He could always climb in through the hole in the roof (they'd none of them dare use the attic now, he'd made sure of that); though he'd have to act fast before that interfering scumbag Gordon began the repairs. However, since he'd had a skinful of ale and wasn't too steady on his feet, he decided to give that idea a miss for tonight. There must be an easier way…

The landlord rang the bell for last orders. Eli lurched up for a final pint, downed it in one then staggered out to roam the deserted streets. He stumbled about for hours, having lost all sense of direction; even tried to let himself into the wrong house and set off a burglar alarm. Finally however, he found himself in the fields up on Cloud Hill. There he collapsed in a stupor and slept fitfully till he was roused in the early hours by a blinding bright light. Thinking it might be police headlights he cowered behind a nearby bush and watched. To his horror, the light grew closer and a huge dome-shaped craft appeared. It hovered a few feet from the ground and then landed silently behind a thicket of trees.

#

Amelie!

Amelie opened her eyes to find no one there. She glanced at her clock and pulled the duvet over her head. 'Four thirty!' She groaned. 'When I said up with the lark I didn't mean this early!'

Amelie, come now! The voice lingered in her head and she pictured herself standing behind the hangar. The thought was so strong she leapt out of bed and drew back the curtains. The sun had already risen.

Meet me here. I'm waiting.

Quickly she pulled on her jeans and a tee-shirt, grabbed the crystal from under her pillow and opened her door, ready to wake Tim. But to her surprise he was already there, up and dressed and tip-toeing towards her room.

'You heard it too?' he whispered.

'Yes, it'll be Dorin, I'm sure. Let's take the back stairs down to the scullery. Less chance we'll be heard that way.'

But, hearing movements, Lara and Freddie were already waiting for them at the foot of the stairs.

'Come on, Freddie!' Amelie said, and went off to fetch his harness.

Tim grabbed her arm. 'No, if Mum comes down early she'll realise we've gone out too.'

'Fine, but what about Isla? We can't go without her.'

Tim glanced at his phone. 'It's only four-forty, too early to call. Let's go to the hangar and see what happens.' He reached up and unbolted the heavy oak door. Hardly anyone used the scullery these days so they could easily slip out unnoticed, leaving the kitchen door safely locked and bolted. Then, just as they were leaving, he remembered.

'The little figures! Shall I go back and get them?'

'No, no,' Amelie said. 'There's bound to be a next time.' And they climbed the stone steps to the garden.

Chapter Twenty-Two

Dorin and the Commander

Outside the morning was bright but cool, the sun not yet high enough in the sky to warm them. Shoulders hunched, they breathed on their hands and hurried through the dew-covered garden. Amelie wished she had worn her fleece jacket but her shivers were more from anticipation than cold. As they neared the hangar, she let out a gasp of surprise. 'Look who's there, it's Isla!'

They rushed towards her. 'That's amazing,' Tim said. 'You heard it too! We were afraid you'd miss him.'

No-chance!

That was Dorin's voice again all right. There was a rustle of leaves and a small figure stepped out from the trees behind the hangar. He raised his hand, bowed deeply and touched his heart.

'I must say, you're getting pretty good at this,' he laughed. His eyes glowed with pleasure. 'Even without a transonometer, you all heard me loud and clear.'

He handed them each a small object, a little like a battery with a tiny screen. 'You've earned one of these, I think. It's the very latest model.'

Tim's eyes lit up. 'Cool, our own transonometer! Will it like translate anything?' French was not his favourite subject at school.

'Not a problem,' Dorin said. *'Pas de problème!'*

'And is it solar-powered?' Isla asked, searching for some kind of USB port.

Amelie turned the little gadget over in her hands. 'What I need to know is, can it spell? That would be such a great help with my books.'

'Slow down!' Dorin hissed. 'Too many questions... Yes, yes, and yes! And, as you'll see, it's very easy to use.' He took his own transonometer and attached it to one ear. 'See, it clips on, like so, and connects with the language centre in your brain. It then changes sound waves and thought waves into recognisable words; very useful in emergencies when telepathy is interrupted...'

'You mean mind-reading?' Amelie asked. 'That's incredible.'

'Yes, I'll show you.' He closed his eyes for a moment and concentrated very hard before removing the transonometer from his ear. An unrecognisable word flashed up on its tiny screen. 'There, that's Zalnean for decimals, Amelie,' he joked. Then his face became serious.

'Now listen, I need you to remember the Commander's words: *Your home is in great danger, and only you can save it.* What is it, Tim?'

'But we have done! We even raised more money than we needed.'

'Yes, I know.' Dorin smiled appreciatively. 'But now you have an even greater challenge. This is precisely why I sent for you.' He beckoned them to follow and soon they were standing once more before the enormous dome-shaped Scoutship.

'Step aboard.' An opening appeared and they found themselves yet again in the little entrance hall. 'This way...' Dorin indicated a passageway to one side and immediately lowered his voice. 'Come through to our meeting room. There is someone here who would very much like to see you.' He put a finger to his lips and signalled for quiet then entered ahead of them and bowed solemnly.

There, in a blaze of light stood Amelie's ten foot tall man, exactly as she remembered him. He was indeed the figure in Aunt Eggy's stained glass window! For a while they all remained silent, overcome by his formidable presence. Should they bow, they wondered? Should they even dare to speak? However, they needn't have worried. He smiled, turned to face Amelie and gave her a knowing wink.

'Well done, my friends! Now, please make yourselves at home...' He indicated three comfortable chairs, arranged in triangular form, and urged them to be seated. 'By the way, although I am known as the Commander, I command no one. Only myself,' he added with a smile. 'You see, we are all commanders of our own actions.' His gaze rested on each one in turn. 'And it's through your own actions, together with a good deal of hard work and imagination, that you have successfully saved Hadleigh House from disaster. Bravo! You may not realise it but this has been of immense service to us, the Earth Watchers.' He then signalled to Dorin. 'Dorin, please continue.'

'Thank you, *Tuló*.' Dorin bowed. 'You see, my friends, *Havenbridge*, or Heaven-bridge as it was once known, is an ancient bridge between Luga and the Heavens. It is a powerful energy centre on your planet; one that for aeons has magnetically drawn visitors from more advanced civilisations in the Cosmos. Hadleigh House was built directly on top of this centre. This enables us to contact and protect you. *Especially*,' he emphasised, 'at ominous times like this...'

Amelie glanced at him warily. 'It's the End of the World, isn't it?'

'That rather depends upon you,' Dorin said gravely.

'Us?'

'Yes, you; don't look so surprised...'

'But why?' Amelie faltered. 'We're only children.'

'Why?' The Commander clapped his long-fingered hands. 'Perhaps because you each have something rather special to offer...' He turned to Dorin who nodded enthusiastically. 'Yes, *Tuló*.'

'As you may know, we've had a very close association with your family for generations. And, as Dorin hinted earlier, you now have a greater task still. Your house under threat is one thing, your home is another.'

They looked at one another in confusion. The Commander was talking in riddles!

'Luga, your planetary home...' He stood up and gestured to a small screen on the wall which lit up to show an image of Planet Earth. 'The magnificent Blue Planet, one of the most beautiful in all creation. However,' he added abruptly, 'she is now in very grave danger.'

They listened in horror, unable to speak. 'Your rivers and oceans have become poisoned, the air hardly fit to breathe; but there is now a further crisis: you Lugans are in possession of the most lethal weapons ever known. There is a very real threat of war. One neither you nor your planet would survive.'

'How would it feel,' asked Dorin, 'to lose the very earth from under your feet?'

Amelie sat on the edge of her seat. 'No!' she cried, becoming more agitated by the minute. 'We have to do something!'

'And you will...' Dorin said gently. He turned to the Commander and touched his arm. 'Excuse me, *Tuló*, why don't we all have some breakfast first?'

The Commander nodded and waved his hand and at once a large table appeared before them. 'We'll continue our conversation later.' He raised his hand again and an assortment of dishes arrived: rainbow-coloured fruits that looked like bananas, little cakes that smelled of roasted chestnuts. 'Please help yourselves!'

They sat, speechless, trying to come to terms with what he had just told them. And now this too, more food than they could ever eat.

Dorin smiled. 'There are those on Luga – *Tulós* or wise beings – who can perform what you still think of as miracles. Yet these are not really miracles at all; it's precisely how we're all meant to live!'

He and the Commander moved lightly as though weightless, despite appearing as solid as they themselves. Their skin was fine, almost translucent. 'We're able to change the vibrational rate of our bodies,' he explained, hearing their thoughts. 'That's how we *seem* to appear and disappear.' Suddenly he vanished, and in the blink of an eye reappeared.

Tim gasped. 'You mean, like those aircraft in Storm's story!'

Just then a jug materialised with five quaint little cups, holding just enough for a mouthful.

'Try some,' Dorin said, 'and tell me if it isn't the most delicious thing you've ever tasted.'

And it was. It tasted like peach (Amelie's guess) and strawberry (Tim's), and possibly mango (Isla's favourite fruit).

'No, it's millienta juice,' Dorin said, producing a small round fruit, the size of a tennis ball. 'A great delicacy on Zalnea.'

The Commander gestured and they all became silent once more. 'Now for your part in our Plan to save Luga…' He rubbed his chin thoughtfully. 'Let's begin with you, Amelie. Firstly, your ability to mind-wander has created a vital portal through which we, the Earth Watchers, may enter. This is of enormous value to us.'

Amelie flushed with pride. *Doorways to hidden worlds;* yes, Storm's words were beginning to make perfect sense.

'You are also our *Communicator* par excellence. Stories are a great way to get across information that people wouldn't otherwise accept. Like your book about Storm, for instance – who would possibly believe those adventures yet they're all absolutely true!' The Commander rested his hand on her shoulder. 'Soon you'll be writing about us, the Earth Watchers!'

A surge of energy rushed through Amelie, followed by a feeling of such intense excitement and happiness that it was all she could do not to burst into peals of laughter. They all felt it, Isla and Tim too, and they laughed until tears rolled down their cheeks.

The Commander beamed. 'Now you, Isla…' He closed his eyes and took a deep breath. 'You are our *Peacemaker*: loving, wise, and honest…' He paused. 'We Watchers do not understand dishonesty, by the way. In fact, it's impossible for us to lie because we already know one another's thoughts. You must all be very careful never to lie…'

Tim shifted in his seat, remembering his dengue fever joke.

'Yes, Isla, you will fly high!' the Commander continued, pretending not to notice. 'How do you fancy piloting one of our ships?'

Isla gasped. 'You bet I would!'

'Good, it shall be arranged.' Then, sensing that Tim was growing rather restless, the Commander turned to him warmly. 'Dear Tim, whatever would we do without you?'

A look of gratitude spread over Tim's face, and Amelie's eyes brimmed with tears for her brother.

'You, Tim, are our *Warrior* - a rock for your family and friends; loyal and courageous.' He laid a hand on Tim's shoulder. 'You've gained much useful knowledge during your time on Luga, my young friend. Yes,' he teased, 'enough to build the biggest high-speed Skyrail on your planet one day!'

Tim opened his mouth but no words would come out. This had to be the happiest day of his life.

'*You, Children of Luga, are the World Changers,*' said the Commander looking at each one in turn. 'Isn't that the most exciting thing you ever heard?'

They sat in awe-filled silence while he continued. 'And the real force for change is a small group like you, working together. *You... you... and you*! A triangle of power...'

It was then that they realised; their seats had been arranged deliberately as a triangle.

'Exactly,' the Commander said, reading their thoughts, 'an *equilateral* triangle!'

'A triangle with sides of equal length,' Tim said. 'And equal angles, sixty degrees.'

The Commander laughed, seeing Amelie's confusion. 'Please don't let it concern you, dear girl. Let's just say this triangle is a perfect symbol for your group. It simply means you are all equal in importance.'

With that he continued to eat his breakfast and bade them do likewise.

Chapter Twenty-Three

Eli Dankstone and the Dark Heart Army

Isla was beginning to fret. It felt like hours had passed since she'd left Cloud Cottage. Her dad and Auntie George would surely be awake by now and would soon notice she'd gone missing. Dorin, sensing her concern, reassured her at once.

'All is well, Isla. Just remember, there is actually no time here; only N-O-W.'

'I shan't keep you, anyway,' the Commander said. 'But I do need to tell you this…

There are those on Luga who crave power and will fight to get it. They are known as *The Dark Heart Army*. Far worse than the most savage of animals they will stop at nothing to get what they want. Were there to be another war on Luga, no life would remain; something the Dark Hearts appear to be oblivious of.'

The Dark Hearts - Magnus's film! Amelie's lip quivered.

'This means that all neighbouring planets are in danger too: Zalnea, Lumea, Trankon, and others. You see, whatever you do on Luga has a significant effect elsewhere, even at a great distance. This is a great Law of Life.'

He pointed to the screen. 'You remember beautiful Luga, your precious home? Now take a look at this:'

Before them, lay a grey and desolate world, deserted with no sign of human habitation; no animals, no trees. Just a dull sky and dried up rivers.

'The legacy of war,' the Commander said quietly. 'Are you willing to save Luga from this possible future?'

'Yes, *Tuló,*' they heard themselves say.

'Excellent. Then I shall explain your tasks in detail when we next meet. Have you anything to add, Dorin?'

'Only this, *Tuló...*' Dorin replied. 'Tim, Amelie, and Isla, you've all been preparing for this for hundreds of years.'

Amelie suddenly felt very small. 'But I'm only ten.'

'And I'm not thirteen till next year,' said Tim.

'I think I understand.' Isla's eyes lit up, as though some great truth had just dawned on her. 'Is this something to do with our having lived before?'

Dorin smiled. 'Indeed. We've all been waiting for this meeting since the day you were born. We recognised you even then as being useful to the Plan and have been keeping watch over you ever since.'

'But *how* did you recognise us?' they cried in unison.

'By your Light,' said the Commander. 'Well, you do rather stand out from the crowd.' He smiled and lifted a lock of Amelie's bright red hair. 'We're not called Earth Watchers for nothing!' He tilted his head. 'Yes, Tim?'

'I want to know more about the Dark Heart Army.'

'The name tells you all you need to know. The Dark Hearts are an ancient group of evildoers. They prevail in virtually every land on Luga.' He lowered his voice. 'And in this case, very close to home.'

Amelie's eyes widened. 'You mean Elias Dankstone, don't you?'

The Commander nodded. 'Yes, and many others like him; they are led by their Masters, the Dark Heart Lords. These are from the Dark Planet, Daktron; the furthest planet from our Sun. Though technologically advanced they have no regard whatsoever for others.'

'Yes,' Dorin said. 'People you would definitely not wish

to meet in a deserted street on a dark night!'

Amelie and Tim exchanged glances, remembering their encounter in Devil's Gulley.

'And because of their love of money and power, those like the Bottomley-Slighs and the Dankstones attract these Dark Forces to them and unwittingly become their servants.'

The Commander drew closer. 'The Dark Hearts recognise neither family nor friendship and will gladly betray one another if it serves their purpose. They are only interested in what they can get.'

A thought of Magnus crossed the children's minds.

'Yes, Magnus has been trained to cheat and betray his own family if necessary. Their minds may be powerful but you each have something they will never possess: a Bright Heart.'

The light in the Scoutship suddenly dimmed and, looking down, they saw themselves shining like beacons in the darkness.

'The Dark Hearts will stop at nothing,' said Dorin. 'Some have significant psychic powers, especially the ability to watch others at a great distance, and know where they are.'

Amelie shuddered. 'I'll never feel safe again.'

'For this reason, Bright Hearts, make sure you are never alone, and carry these always.' The Commander opened his hand and revealed two small, multi-faceted objects: bright blue, and veined with gold. 'Lumeanite crystals from the sacred mountains of Holos. They have special powers of protection and healing. Here, take them; they will help to keep you safe.'

Tim and Isla examined them closely.

'What about Amelie's?' Isla asked.

'She has one already.'

Amelie's cheeks were on fire. 'Tim, Isla, I'm sorry, the Commander gave it to me that day on the stairs. I really wanted to tell you both but...'

The Commander stopped her. 'No, no, Amelie, it was a test, and you passed it with flying colours. You have proved yourself to be trustworthy; to keep silent when necessary, even before those you love.'

Amelie took the little crystal from her pocket, relieved that her secret was out at last.

'Each crystal has the power to keep you invisible from prying eyes, but for this to happen you must concentrate on it intently.'

Invisible! How wonderful that will be… Amelie squeezed her crystal and focussed hard.

'Where are you, Amelie? You don't need to hide from me!' the Commander joked. He moved from one to the next, his hand resting on each head in turn. They felt a great surge of energy pass through them, as though they had become inflated, and were now as tall as the Commander himself. His enormous eyes twinkled. 'And, don't forget, my dear Brother and Sisters, while there are children like you on this planet, what can possibly go wrong?' Then he stopped abruptly and a look of concern passed over his tranquil face. He murmured something incomprehensible in Dorin's ear and the two Earth Watchers exchanged glances.

'Is something wrong?' Isla asked apprehensively.

'You must leave at once!' Dorin spoke hurriedly and ushered them at great speed through the control room and into the small entrance hall. 'And don't forget to keep your crystals on you at all times.'

Tim checked his phone. It was nearly four fifty. They had only left the house ten minutes ago. 'How did all that happen in no time at all?'

'Have you forgotten?' Dorin said. 'Only on Luga are you bound by time. There's only N-O-W, this eternal moment.'

'No time,' Amelie murmured wistfully. She was back once more on the harbour wall, watching the little boats, and thinking how time seemed to have dropped anchor too.

Dorin waved them off briskly. 'Go quickly now, Bright Hearts, and meet me in three days, before sunrise. I'll have another surprise for you then.'

Chapter Twenty-Four

Amelie in Danger

'I wonder what the emergency is,' Tim said. 'I guess I'd better run on ahead; I've left the scullery door unlocked.'

'I must go too.' Isla blew them a kiss and hurried off through the garden, gripping her piece of Lumeanite so no one would spot her on the way home.

Amelie followed, searching in her jeans pocket for her crystal. It had been there a moment ago but she'd forgotten the little hole in her pocket; one she'd been meaning to mend for weeks. As she ran it made its way down her leg, lodged itself in her trainers and finally fell free.

'Tim, Isla – wait! I've lost my Stone of Power!' But they were both already out of earshot. She fell to her knees, groping around in the long grass.

A bird landed on a nearby branch. She continued her search until at last she felt it under her palm. Just like Storm had when he landed safely in the field! But her relief was short-lived for beyond the rose bush was a small movement; a fleeting shadow and crackle of twigs. Her body stiffened as she remembered the Commander's words: *make sure you are never alone!* She sneezed, and glanced around anxiously, sensing someone close. Then, before she could even begin to focus on the crystal to save her, she clambered wildly to her feet and tried to let out a scream.

From within his foxhole up on Cloud Hill Eli Dankstone had watched, wide-eyed, as the great dome-shaped craft landed. A small figure jumped out; the weirdest little guy he'd ever seen. Moments later another figure joined him, then two more. 'Yes,' he muttered, 'the brats from the house!'

He'd lain there for a while, befuddled; then decided to take a proper look at the old man's shed; snoop around for an entrance to the tunnels. He moved as steadily as ten pints of ale would allow, clambered over the fence, and found himself inside the Trotts' garden. Just as he was peering through the window of the hangar, footsteps approached and he swiftly took cover once more. He listened carefully and reached into his jacket for something to cover his face; the old mask he'd found on the Ballroom floor.

Then suddenly things looked up. The Trott girl was too slow to keep up with the rest. She stumbled and fell, searching around in the grass for (he could hardly believe his ears) *her Stone of Power!*

He moved stealthily from one bush to the next; then emerged silently...

'Got you!' He clamped a hand over her mouth to contain her scream and with the other he prised open her fist and seized the Stone.

A door opened and footsteps approached once more. The lad was returning and ahead of him a dog barked furiously. But he held onto the girl, enjoying his moment of drunken victory; until he stopped abruptly and let out a cry. It wasn't the yapping dog that alarmed him, it was something else. Demonic, howling like a banshee, its green eyes glinted in the undergrowth. It flew at him, latched onto his shoulder, holding fast, until in terror he released his grip and the little Stone fell from his palm.

'Who'd have thought it?' Amelie gasped. 'Eli Dankstone, scared of a tiny fur-ball like Freddie!'

'You mean it was him?' said Tim. 'All I could see was the

mask.'

'I could smell him; he made me sneeze.'

'Lara was howling like crazy. The second I opened the door she was off.'

'She must have known I was in trouble.'

'Freddie too, he puffed himself up to three times his size!'

'Come here, my clever boy!' Amelie gathered Freddie in her arms and kissed him. 'You stopped my Stone of Power from falling into the wrong hands. Now, where's that Lara gone?'

Lara was standing guard at the entrance to the fields.

'Here, girl, he's gone now!' Tim whistled and she ran towards him. 'Let's get you two little heroes some breakfast. We'll have a word with Storm later, but first I'll contact Sergeant Buggeley.'

'No, Tim,' Amelie said firmly. 'We'd only have to explain why we were in the garden so early and Mum's bound to ask a lot of awkward questions and you know we can't lie…'

'I guess so. And we don't want to ruin the rest of Isla's stay.'

'Dorin said to meet him in three days' time so actually that's perfect! Wednesday is when Mum's in London with the gallery people. She's staying overnight so there'll only be Storm here.'

'Maybe he'd like to join us…'

'We'll ask him. And tell him our news…'

'Make sure you mend that pocket, Amelie. That was a warning for us all, I think.'

#

'Thank heavens you're safe,' Storm said. 'You really must be more vigilant.' He squinted at Amelie over the top of his glasses. 'Where's young Isla?'

Amelie's face grew downcast. 'At Cloud Cottage, helping Auntie George. Time's going so quickly since the Sale. We still haven't planned her special trip.'

Privately, Tim was desolate too. 'At least we're all seeing Dorin on Wednesday.'

'You'll come with us this time, won't you, Storm?' Amelie pleaded, tugging at his arm. 'The Commander has a special job for us all.'

The old man's face lit up. 'Carrying on the family tradition then? Well, maybe I will, my dear, though I do have to keep an eye on this place too while your mother's away.' He also had his work cut out in the hangar, planning a little surprise for Isla, and wanted to be sure his little aircraft was in perfect working order. All the same, it would be simply splendid to see his old Earth Watcher friend again.

As it turned out, another surprise had already been planned. Isla had permission to stay over at Hadleigh on Tuesday night and they all decided to be very sensible and grown up and go to bed no later than nine. It felt a lot like Christmas Eve, Amelie said, only far more exciting. Even without the presents.

'Hardly slept a wink,' Storm confessed the next morning, brewing his breakfast coffee. 'Better make this a strong one, I think.'

All the same, they'd never seen him so bright-eyed and alive. He was wearing his best suit and had even trimmed his moustache for the occasion.

'You were looking a bit like a walrus!' Amelie admitted.

He raised his eyebrows in horror. 'Lord, I hope not! My grandfather was known as the Walrus; Theodore, terrifying man!'

It was not yet dawn when they finally set out on their trek through the long, shadowy garden. Tim went slightly ahead with his torch. 'Got everything, guys? Lumeanite?'

'*Check!*' they all shouted.

'Doors locked? (*Check!* I made sure I did this time.)'

'Treats for Freddie and Lara?' Amelie said, tugging on Lara's lead. '*Check! Check!* I put some in my pockets.'

'What about those figures of Dorin and the Commander

you told me about?' asked Isla.

Tim raised his thumb in response. '*Check!*'

'Yes, yes!' Storm said impatiently. 'Come along now, quick march - and careful of any snails on the path!'

It was Storm who spotted Dorin first. He waved his stick which had a little light at the tip and Dorin, recognising his old friend at once, approached swiftly, his big eyes glowing.

'Storm! My-dear-brother...'

The two men greeted each other warmly; each raised a hand in salute, then placed it on his heart and bowed.

There were tears of joy in the old man's eyes. 'Just a flying visit, I'm afraid, pun not intended.' He rested his hands on Dorin's shoulders. 'Is it really you, Dorin? Look at you, still just a boy!' He patted his own balding head. 'Whereas me...'

Dorin laughed. 'But you're a Lugan, Storm. Doing rather well for your age, all the same...' He led them aboard the Scoutship where they let Lara and Freddie off their leads.

Once inside the control room Dorin touched the rear wall and it opened out into a comfortable, softly lit space with a big table in the centre.

'This will be our lunch later.' The table was heaving with unusual dishes; a rainbow selection of fruits and vegetables. 'We'll hook up with our Mothership shortly. How's that with you, Isla? Somewhere you've never been before - a cruise around the Solar Ocean!'

Isla frowned. 'Really? But how long will that take?'

'No-time-at-all...' Dorin made his odd little hissing sound as he always did when he was amused. He sounded rather like a steam iron. He turned and glanced over his shoulder. 'Here come Sorriel and Thula, our pilots. They'll be accompanying us on the Mothership.'

Two young girls entered the room and rushed over to greet Storm. 'We've heard so much about you! You are a renowned Lugan hero on our planets...'

Storm looked like he was about to tell them not to talk

such nonsense but instead allowed himself a moment of pride.

'I'm Sorriel from Zalnea, like Dorin,' the smaller of the two girls said, running her fingers through her shiny dark hair. 'And this,' she said pointing to her very tall and blonde companion, 'is my friend Thula from Lumea, the Commander's planet.'

Both girls gave the Earth Watchers' salute and bowed low, and Storm and the children did the same.

'Well, why don't we all sit down?' Thula held out her hand to Freddie who, having sniffed it carefully leapt onto her lap. Lara flopped down at her feet. 'I love animals,' she said. 'I have many at home.'

'They don't look a bit like aliens, do they?' Isla whispered to Tim.

'Maybe because they're not,' Tim said loudly enough for the Earth Watchers to hear. 'They're just kind of human like us, I suppose.'

'Human?' laughed Storm. 'Humans maybe, but not like us! We Lugans still have a lot to learn.'

'You're right, I'm afraid,' said Sorriel. 'We Earth Watchers come from all over the Cosmos. Most are like us, Zalneans and Lumeans, though our brothers and sisters from Trankon are a little... shall we say, different, as you'll see later. Lumeans are the most advanced race of all,' she added, glancing at Thula.

Amelie listened, enthralled. 'How big is the universe then?'

Storm smiled. 'Which one do you mean, Amelie dear? There are worlds upon worlds; universes upon universes. There's no bigger mystery...'

'Quite right,' Dorin said. 'For some reason, you Lugans believe you're the most advanced beings in the cosmos - the only human life indeed! Ha!' He made his steam iron noise again.

Thula and Sorriel joined in, laughing hysterically.

Meanwhile, Isla longed for an answer to the most impossible question of all: 'Okay, then who exactly made it all?' To which Dorin, Thula and Sorriel all bowed deeply and chorused: 'The Ancient Eternal One!'

For a while, a great hush fell over the little party then Storm and Dorin began to chat animatedly about old times until, overcome by tiredness and excitement, Storm finally closed his eyes and began to snore. Eventually, Dorin rose to his feet and shook him awake. 'Storm, I'm afraid we must prepare for take-off now and hook up with our Mothership.'

'Oh dear, I must have dropped off.' Storm rubbed his eyes and picked up his stick. 'Then sadly, that is my cue to leave you.' He reached out to Dorin who took his hand and pulled him to his feet.

'If you must, but remember we're always close by.' With this promise Dorin placed his hand on Storm's shoulder and guided him out of the craft. 'Don't worry; I'll take care of the Bright Hearts. Just you stay safe now, old friend!'

'I will.'

Outside, Storm turned and waved his walking stick, watching wistfully as the enormous Scoutship rose into the air and swiftly disappeared into the clouds.

Chapter Twenty-Six

A Cruise around the Solar Ocean

'What I don't understand,' Tim said boldly, 'is why you saved Storm's life but not our dad's.'

'Or the others,' Amelie added, thinking of That Terrible Day.

Dorin gave this some careful thought. 'Well, firstly, Storm was badly needed on Luga at that time. Like Eggy, he was part of a useful group of contactees. And secondly...' He hesitated, as though choosing his words carefully. 'The others were needed elsewhere...'

Tim frowned. 'Needed elsewhere - you mean they didn't actually die?'

Dorin nodded. 'Not exactly; you see, after the *accident* we took them home.' He said accident like it wasn't really one at all.

'Home?'

'Yes, with us.' And noting their puzzled expressions he continued. 'The truth is we're always alive! Dying simply means we pass out of our old bodies and carry on living somewhere completely different...'

'You see, Tim,' said Thula, 'we Earth Watchers don't think of death as you do. It's rather like changing into a new set of clothes. One day, you'll see what we mean; for now though, get ready, we're about to dock.'

They had already reached the Mothership, a giant space vessel that was about to carry them far beyond the Moon. Dorin eased the Scoutship into the Mothership's hangar where a passageway opened up to take them aboard. 'This ship is even bigger than Hadleigh House so there'll be plenty of room to explore. Follow me.'

'We are now in the Control Room,' Sorriel said, indicating an enormous screen that filled the whole wall. 'From here you'll be able to view a three-dimensional close-up of life on other planets.'

'Will we land there?' Amelie asked.

Thula, who sat at the control panel, shook her head. 'No, no, you can't leave the ship. Your germs would be far too dangerous.'

Isla looked puzzled. 'So how come you can visit us, Dorin?'

'We've had time to build up resistance,' he replied. 'But we have to go through an intense period of cleansing once we return to our home planets.'

'Not all our people are permitted to land on Luga,' Thula explained. Only those we call *Tulós*, or Commanders, and their assistants.'

'Like you?'

'Yes, we're rather like your diplomats in foreign lands.'

'My mom works with diplomats at the British Embassy in Washington DC,' Isla said proudly.

Dorin nodded. 'We know, Isla. She is most valuable to our work in saving Luga.'

'Really?' Isla's eyes shone. 'You mean, Mom *knows* about you!'

'Indirectly.' He smiled. 'Let's say she's gradually becoming more open to us, less afraid.'

Isla thought about this for a moment. Her mother had never said a word; and as if Dorin had heard her, which indeed he had, he replied:

'And for now you must *all* remain silent too. Talk to no one, apart from Storm.'

'Although one day you'll tell the world about us,' Sorriel added. 'And don't look so surprised; this will be sooner than you think!'

'Watch the screen, everyone - we're fast approaching Zalnea!' Thula called over her shoulder. 'How do you fancy being my co-pilot, Isla?'

Isla was ecstatic. 'Awesome! My first actual flying lesson...'

The others watched as they made their descent. Zalnea wasn't at all like they'd imagined. The cities were more like villages, quite small and carefully laid out with buildings unlike any they'd ever seen before: beautiful, curved edifices, white mainly with pale, shell-like façades, and domed, with no hard edges or harsh angles. There were trees and flowers and lakes everywhere so it was difficult to know really whether they were in the town or the countryside.

They hovered over this strange new world where people went about unhurriedly, as though they had all the time in the world.

'Doesn't anyone go to work?' Amelie asked.

Dorin laughed. 'We work far less than you do but achieve so much more! And since we don't compete with one another we have no stress. What's up then, Tim? You look surprised.'

'No competition? How does that work then?'

'Well, for one thing, we have no use for money. Everything on our planet is free. Why would we want to tire ourselves out, slaving to get things we already have?'

'Our leisure time is very important to us too,' Sorriel explained. 'I'm an artist when I'm not in charge of a Mothership.'

'Sounds like heaven,' Amelie said.

'It is, Amelie. But then heaven is always of our own

making. First though, you Lugans have to grow up!'

'I don't ever want to grow up,' Amelie said firmly. 'Where's the fun in being old?'

Dorin raised an eyebrow. 'Growing up isn't about growing old. It's about becoming wise.'

They all fell silent as they pondered on his words. How wise Dorin was, exceptionally so for someone who looked barely older than themselves.

'Oh wow!' Amelie gasped, gazing up at the big three-dimensional screen. Little flying machines had appeared above them; vehicles like the hovercraft they'd once travelled on from Southsea to Ryde in the Isle of Wight. But these were suspended high in the air, and piloted - by children!

'We develop rather more quickly than you do,' Dorin explained. 'But there's one huge difference between us...' He studied their faces intently. 'You see, Bright Hearts, we no longer suffer as you do.'

'We did once, it seems,' said Sorriel, 'but that was aeons ago. No one can remember such a time though we do have legends about it; terrible wars and turmoil, famines and floods; almost impossible to imagine now.'

Chapter Twenty-Seven

Zolos, the Trankon Guide

They left Zalnea and sailed on through the Waves of Space to Planet Trankon where they paused for an early lunch.

'We're very honoured to have a renowned Trankon Earth Watcher on board with us today,' Dorin announced. 'And hopefully the Commander will join us too. Ah, yes, I think I can hear *Tuló* now…'

'People on other planets look pretty much alike,' the Commander explained over lunch, 'though many are smaller than you.'

Smaller! Tim stared at him in amazement.

The Commander read his thoughts and smiled. 'Yes, well, Lumea is an exception. Anyway,' he winked, 'I've been around for many thousands of years. Enough time to have grown rather tall.'

'Isla, please come and join us now.' Dorin patted the empty seat beside him then filled their tiny cups with millienta juice. 'All over the Cosmos there is human life; most share a certain likeness but vary in stature, skin colour, and so on. However, the race that developed on Planet Trankon is somewhat special…' (He decided he'd better warn the young Lugans in advance.) 'They have developed a single eye.'

At that very moment, a new Earth Watcher entered the

room with a number of others behind him.

Dorin bowed deeply. 'This is Zolos, a very ancient and esteemed Trankon guide.'

'*Tuló!*' The Trankon guide bowed first to the Commander, then to Dorin and the two young pilots. Finally, he turned to the others and peered at them sharply with his enormous all-seeing eye. It dominated his old face. 'Slantora?'

Even without consulting their transonometers they all knew exactly what he was asking.

'Timothy,' Tim answered at once, introducing himself.

'Slantora zonta?'

'Timothy Michael Trott.'

Zolos wobbled his head then turned to Isla. 'Slantora zonta?'

'Isla Jane Batty,' she replied. Incredible! They could all understand quite easily.

Amelie, however, was deeply concerned about her middle name. It was now her turn and the Commander had told them they must never ever lie.

'Amelie J. Trott.'

'Boaji? J - pa?' (What kind of name is that? J?')

She couldn't possibly reply. Even Isla, her closest friend, still didn't know. How could she say it *without actually* saying it? How amazing just to be ordinary like everyone else with an ordinary name such as Amelie Jade or Jenna; anything rather than …

And suddenly she felt guilty for being so ashamed of her dead grandma's name; Grandma Joan, who'd been such a kind and special lady. 'Jo-an,' she mumbled, looking at her feet. 'Amelie Jo-an Trott.'

'*Na, Joan!*' corrected Zolos, his great eye twinkling. He looked less severe suddenly, and his retinue turned to one another, wobbling their heads from side to side which, Dorin explained, was the Trankon way of nodding.

Just like Mrs Patel, Isla remembered.

There were many famous Joans in the Trankon encyclopedia of Luga's history, Zolos explained, though none greater than Joan of Arc, the famous French heroine and saint.

Amelie still looked doubtful. 'I suppose…'

Zolos winked though it was more of a blink due to him having only one eye.

'Ek Joan! Sjalzi duuray? (Perhaps you will be the next famous Joan?)

'Joan!' Isla whispered. 'What a beautiful name!'

Suddenly, Amelie wished she'd never given her autograph book away.

And, without knowing why, Tim reached into his pocket and there it was - Amelie's autograph book! Yet he'd seen it that very morning, inside the second drawer down of his bedside table. He turned to his sister who was looking every bit as astonished as he was. 'Here, this is yours. I was only kidding about your secret being safe. Not that it was much of a secret anyway; only a name. And yes, Isla's right, I think Joan's a really cool name too.'

Amelie clutched her precious little book and opened it at random. There, right beneath *Robbie Williams*, Dorin had signed his name too! And where there had been blank pages before there were others, names she didn't even recognise; all part of a future as yet to be revealed…

Chapter Twenty-Eight
The Planet of No Goodbyes

'So, Bright Hearts, now for the final stage of our journey!' The Commander announced, 'Lumea, Planet of No Goodbyes! Will you join us, Thula?'

'What an amazing name for a planet,' Amelie said. She felt like a great weight had been lifted from her shoulders. Not only did she have her autograph book once more, she was free to be herself at last; her whole self – Amelie Joan Trott!

'And what a beautiful place it is too!' Isla breathed, her eyes fixed on the three-dimensional screen. 'Every single building looks like a temple...' Homes, schools, and store-houses, all were built in the same graceful style, fashioned out of what looked to be shimmering white marble.

'That's because everything and everyone is sacred to us,' Thula said. 'You'll notice we have no shops? Just stores where we collect whatever we need: food, clothing, TV sets, and so on. There is always more than enough to share.'

'Lumea...' Tim watched in amazement. 'It's like we're actually *there*.'

'Look there!' Amelie cried. 'A horse with wings...' And as she spoke, it began to canter, and picking up speed it ascended and flew gracefully above the rooftops.

There were other flying creatures there too: fabulous

birds with translucent wings; sparrows like parrots, brightly coloured like everything else on this extraordinary planet.

'I see you like animals.' Thula smiled approvingly. Freddie stretched and gave his little slow-blink smile. 'Why don't we let these two explore?'

Lara's tail began to quiver and she ran to fetch her lead.

'What do you say, Dorin? They'll come to no harm.'

'As long as they're back in time for their first assignment. Lara, Freddie!' Dorin stood up and ushered them into a long corridor. 'Off you go…'

'I'll show you my own pets now,' Thula said. The screen flickered and an image appeared of two small, furry rabbit-like creatures.

'Meet Kitchi and Khula. These two little creatures have developed a high degree of mental ability.'

'They're so cute!' said Isla. 'Hey, Kitchi and Kuhla, I'm taking you home…'

There were larger animals too, roaming freely in fields and pastureland. 'We Lumeans have no need for animals as food. Rabbits, sheep, cows, and pigs – all have evolved much like your own but we like to keep them as friends. We get great pleasure from our animal companions, don't we Tuló?'

The Commander nodded. 'Indeed, Thula, and like our friend Storm, we grow everything we need - plants, vegetables, and fruits – though we Tulós can also manifest food when needed, as you saw earlier…' He closed his eyes and with a click of his fingers a large pumpkin-like vegetable appeared on the table before them.

'Try some.' He cut it into slices and handed it around. They all agreed it tasted a lot like a juicy, ripe peach.

At that moment Dorin returned and Tim remembered the two small figures he had in his pocket. 'We've been waiting to show you these,' he said, placing them in Dorin's hand. Storm thinks our dad may have made them when he was a boy.'

'Michael?' Dorin's eyes glowed. 'Here, look, *Tuló!* These are you and me…'

The Commander laughed. 'How very timely, my friends. This leads me perfectly to our next surprise. Do you remember a dream you had once, Amelie – the one where you saw a bright planet?'

Amelie caught her breath. 'Yes, I do!' She had told no one. It had been the most extraordinary dream, one she would certainly never forget. High in the sky a star or a planet shone brightly. It was so detailed she might have been looking through some giant telescope, like the one they'd once seen at Jodrell Bank Discovery Centre. She could even make out on its surface a number of people gazing down at her. They reminded her rather of the figures in Aunt Eggy's stained glass window, but these were all alive and waving eagerly to her. They looked so warm and friendly that the most wonderful feeling of peace came over her, an excited peace, she remembered, and she'd waved back; shyly at first, then boldly, and this seemed to bring the figures to life even more!

'It was almost like they knew me,' Amelie said. 'And I could see their faces quite clearly.'

The Commander smiled. 'That was Lumea, Planet of No Goodbyes.'

'And did you know,' Dorin said, 'that people who have died can sometimes contact you in dreams?' He paused. 'Well, it's time to meet another Earth Watcher now...'

A group of Earth Watchers appeared on the screen, all wearing robes emblazoned with the now familiar symbol of hands cupped around a globe. The tallest of these stepped forward and bent towards them, just as though he was standing in the room. He had very light blonde hair, worn long like the Commander's. He spoke softly. 'Hello, Timmy!'

Tim blinked. No one had called him Timmy for years.

'And you, little Amelie Joan…'

Without turning her head, Amelie flashed a sideways glance at her brother. The Earth Watcher had the saddest look in his eyes, the kind of look that usually ended in tears. His big green eyes glistened and the children had a sudden urge to rush forward and comfort him. But then he smiled.

'These are tears of joy, my children. Don't you see? It's just *me*, in a new set of clothes!'

Astonished, they remembered Thula's words. For although his hair was blonde, the Earth Watcher's face was very familiar. He was the man in their mother's studio; the painting really had come to life!

Dad! Tim stared at him mutely.

'Yes, Tim, I'm very *much* alive!'

'Cool,' Isla murmured, 'how awesome is that!'

'Yes, Isla, you're now part of our family too. Believe me - you have many more awesome adventures ahead of you…' He turned his attention to Tim and Amelie once more. 'How very proud of you I am! You know, I've tried to contact you so many times, to warn you about the Bottomley-Slighs… But it was you, Tim, who heard me. Do you remember that dream?'

Tim nodded. It was the railway dream, the one he'd been reluctant to share. It was all beginning to make sense at last. No wonder he'd made those little Earth Watchers models so well; their father was one of them, too!

And picking up on his thoughts, Michael produced another small figure out of nowhere, a painted model of Yoda, the Jedi Master.

'Your model,' Amelie gasped, 'but that one's in Storm's desk, locked inside a drawer with little brass handles!'

'And that's precisely where you'll find it when you return.' He raised his hand in the Earth Watchers' salute. 'Now, please forgive me but I'm needed elsewhere. Tell your beautiful mother how much I love her…' He looked at

Amelie and winked. 'I only ever want her to live her life and be happy. And lastly, remember all of you, there really are no goodbyes, neither here nor on Luga. You will always find me in your dreams...' And with that the screen went blank.

Amelie and Tim looked at each other in shock. 'You do realise what this means,' Tim murmured.

'Yes,' said Amelie, 'we have Earth Watchers' blood!'

Chapter Twenty-Nine
It's Down to You, Children of Luga!

'So, now that you know the truth,' the Commander said solemnly, 'you must never forget who you are…' And, not wishing to leave Isla out: 'Are you enjoying your special trip, my young friend?'

Isla was lost for words. 'What can I say? It's been absolutely…'

'Arsum?' Amelie mimicked.

The Commander threw back his head and laughed heartily. Then, composing himself, he studied their faces. 'Do you have any further questions before we leave?'

Isla thought for a moment. 'Yes, why is it you guys can't visit us openly, so everyone can see you?'

'A very good question, Isla. Well, think of it this way; just as some Lugans dislike foreign people, imagine how much harder they'd find it to accept beings from other planets, especially those of us who look significantly different to themselves. Ten foot tall creatures, monsters with one eye…'

'They wouldn't even deign to call us people.' Thula shook her head. 'Aliens indeed!'

'Imagine this,' Dorin said, 'many of us have been living amongst you, unrecognised, for aeons. Over time we have been able to adapt enough to pass as Lugans. Your Aunt Eglantyne knew this; Michael was one, others also…'

'Is nice Mr Goodman one?' Amelie asked.

Dorin smiled. 'No, just an ordinary Lugan with a very kind heart; he recognises a deep bond with you all. Do we have time for one more question, *Tuló?*'

'Just one.'

Tim raised his hand as though he were in school. 'What about the tunnels under our house? Is there really any gold hidden there?'

Dorin shook his head. 'The items contained within those passages are actually more precious than gold. One day they'll be of great interest to your historians, isn't that right, *Tuló?*'

'Yes, but only once Lugans accept the fact that we extra-terrestrials exist. As Storm will have told you, the tunnels had to be sealed. Why? Because The Dark Hearts had got too close to discovering them and would have used them for their own evil purposes. Watch this…' The screen now showed Storm in his hangar, merrily tinkering with his beloved flying machine.

'There's a secret entrance right there…' Dorin pointed to a spot right under the aircraft. 'See? A little trapdoor with steps leading down to the tunnels; the exit is in your basement scullery. Even Storm doesn't know its exact location yet.'

'Pity they're all sealed off,' Tim said.

'We created them as a means of contacting Eglantyne safely and for assisting with her projects. You'll learn more about these in years to come. For now there are projects of your own to consider.'

'Yes, indeed!' The Commander had begun to pace up and down the room. 'We're increasingly concerned about the escalation of weapons on Luga. Created and funded by the Dark Hearts, they are the most deadly the world has ever known. Unless they are deactivated at once, your planet is doomed.' He paused to let his words sink in… 'And so also are we, your planetary neighbours: Zalnea, Trankon and Lumea.' Then, seeing such alarm on their faces, he spoke more gently:

'Forgive me for causing fear in your hearts but your leaders are intent on gathering a stockpile of these evil weapons, believing they will protect Luga from harm. Yet nothing is further from the truth!'

Filled with a sudden rage, Amelie banged her fist on the table just like Storm sometimes did. 'But that's terrible, we must stop them! Right now...'

'Yes, since the adults of the world can be no longer trusted to safeguard the future of your planet, I'm afraid it's down to you, *Children of Luga!*' The Commander's eyes flashed with a force so sudden they shielded their eyes.

Children of Luga! They stared at one another, unable to take in the enormity of the Commander's proposal. They'd already rescued Hadleigh House; now all they had to do was save their planet!

'Yes,' Tim said hoarsely, 'but how, that's the question?'

'Well, Bright Hearts, I propose a plan, one that will put your imagination and ingenuity to the test once more.' He smiled fondly at the little group before him. 'This is your task: you are to change the hearts and minds of those in power!'

'You mean speak to the *Prime Minister?*' Amelie said, wondering if this might be stretching her own powers of communication a little too far.

'No one ever gets to talk to the President,' said Isla, sensing that this part might well be down to her. 'Not even my mom.'

'Ah, but you can reach them indirectly,' the Commander said mysteriously. 'And the most reliable way to achieve this is to let them come into contact with a piece of this...' He produced two tiny pieces of rose pink crystal and gave one to Amelie and the other to Isla. 'Shalamite, from the heart of

Lumea's sacred caves.'

'Remember,' Dorin hinted, 'not all in government are Lords of War. There are others who quietly have influence in the Halls of Power. Like your mom, Isla; wise beings all over Luga who are dedicated to Peace.' His eyes glowed and he hissed like a steam iron again. 'And not all of them are human...'

'I'll give you a further clue,' the Commander said. 'The Downing Street Cat...'

The children frowned. The Commander was talking in riddles again!

But very soon a look of recognition spread over Amelie's face. 'Larry!' she said. Tim and Isla watched her, bemused. 'Chief Mouser to the Cabinet...'

Chapter Thirty

The Downing Street Cat and the White House Dogs

'You mean we're actually going to Number Ten?' Isla hooted. 'To *see a cat?* I'm sorry, but I don't understand…'

'Well,' Amelie explained, 'I do know the Prime Minister quite likes Larry, the famous Downing Street cat. If we could just hide this around his neck somehow…' She opened her palm and examined the little pink crystal. 'See, Isla, it's vibrating. Can you feel it?'

'Yes,' said Isla, 'and there are beams of light radiating from it too… Beautiful, isn't it?'

'Got it!' Tim grinned. 'The Prime Minister strokes the cat and comes into direct contact with the crystal…'

Dorin's face lit up. 'Exactly! The Shalamite will prepare your Prime Minister for a powerful change of heart.'

'Likewise with the White House dogs,' the Commander continued. 'Yes, Isla; you are to open the President's heart.' He smiled, seeing the look of dismay on her face. 'Impossible is *not* a word we Earth Watchers understand.'

Dorin leapt to his feet. 'We'd better summon Lara and Freddie for their next mission then. No time like the present!'

'No time at all,' they all chorused, beginning at last to understand.

Dorin dropped them all off in St. James's Park, quite close to their destination. 'See you back here; till then, I'd better make myself invisible.' And with that he was gone in a flash.

'Shall I do it then?' Amelie asked, hoping Tim would say no and snatch it from her.

'Yes, go on,' said Tim. 'You're good at that kind of thing.'

'What?' She'd never done "that kind of thing" in her life. 'Okay, since the future of the human race is at stake, I will.' She took a small piece of elastic she'd found in her pocket and began to thread it through a tiny hole in the crystal. 'Let's just hope Larry's there. Lara, Freddie, let's go - we have a world to save!'

They arrived at a set of imposing black iron gates that blocked their entry to Downing Street. There, a rather severe looking policeman greeted them and eyed Amelie suspiciously. 'Good afternoon, Madam. No entry to the public, I'm afraid.'

'Hello, officer, I'm looking for Larry, the Prime Minister's cat. I hope he's well….' Nerves had overcome her and she started to gabble. She took a deep breath to slow herself down.

He looked down at the small girl and sniffed. 'I am a police officer, Madam, not a veterinary surgeon.'

Amelie had never been called Madam before but decided she'd have to get used to it once she was a world-famous writer, and this gave her the very idea she needed. 'I'm writing an article called "Famous People and their Pets." The words tumbled out before she could stop them. Now she really would have to write that article, remembering what the Commander had said about telling lies. She felt in her pocket and pulled out a little packet of Freddie's favourite cat treats and began to rattle it. Freddie glanced up hopefully.

What a very strange girl. The police officer shaded his eyes with his hands, pretending to look for the cat. 'Well, well, as luck would have it, here he is now,' he said suddenly.

The cat from Number Ten had appeared out of nowhere, stepped through a gap in the railings and was now rubbing around their legs. 'Would you like to interview him then, Madam?'

Isla giggled. 'Are all English policemen like this?'

'He's barking mad,' said Tim.

Amelie shot them a warning glance. 'Shut up! You'll get us arrested.' She turned to the policeman and smiled. 'No thank you, officer. A photo will do. Come here, Larry!' She offered the cat a couple of treats and tried to remain calm.

The policeman turned his head, attempting to maintain his dignified demeanour. Meanwhile, Amelie slipped the tiny crystal necklace over Larry's head and deftly concealed the elastic under his fur. 'Good boy, Larry...' She picked him up while Tim reached through the gates with his mobile phone. 'Thank you, officer. Now, would you mind just taking a couple of photos of us?'

'You nailed it!' said Tim and Amelie beamed, surprised at how easy it had been. She felt she had grown several inches since leaving home that morning; in confidence too. It was not quite midday but they had already eaten lunch, visited two planets, and accomplished one world changing mission. A hop across the Atlantic seemed like nothing after that.

'Excellent!' Dorin said. 'So, next stop the White House?'

'I only hope I do half as well as you, Amelie,' Isla said, fidgeting nervously with her piece of Shalamite.

'Of course you will!' chorused Tim and Amelie.

'I found this tiny ball of Blu Tack in my pocket, left over from the Sale. It should stick the crystal to a dog's collar okay.'

It was still early morning when they touched down in Washington DC and Isla remembered that the President's aides took the dogs for their daily walk around seven.

'We'll try to wait here,' Dorin said. 'Just give us a buzz when you're ready. Transonometer?'

'Check!' said Isla.

'Shalamite?'

'Check!'

'Off you go then, and break an arm!'

'That's not very nice,' Amelie said.

'He means *break a leg*,' Tim laughed. 'It's what you say to actors before a performance, to wish them good luck...'

Dorin began to hiss like a steam iron again.

'Oh,' said Amelie. 'But, that's even worse. Anyway, take a few of Lara's biscuits with you, Isla...'

Isla went off to wait by the White House railings, wishing fervently she could call her mom. She'd be getting ready for work now and soon be making her way from Georgetown to the Embassy.

Suddenly, a side door opened and a woman emerged with two little dogs on leads. Isla took a deep breath. Here we go...

'Excuse me, ma'am,' she called. 'My mom, Bettina Rivas, works at the British Embassy. She said I'd find you here with the dogs.'

The woman strode over and looked her up and down warily.

'I've brought them some biscuits...' Isla's hands shook as she placed a couple on her palm. One of the two small dogs pressed forward eagerly.

'The President doesn't want them fed,' the woman snapped ungraciously. 'Too fat as it is. I'd lose my job.'

'Oh, but they're so cute. Could I just stroke them?' Isla reached through the railings to pat their heads.

'Not allowed...'

'Just a photo then?' Isla took out her phone.

'Not allow...' Just then there was a great roar high above them and they both looked up. Dorin was creating a distraction, just as he had all those years ago during the war. Isla wasted no time and quickly reached out to the nearest dog and embedded the tiny crystal under his collar. 'Smile please,' she said brightly and took a photograph of the disgruntled aide as she dragged the two little dogs away.

'Excellent!' The Commander said as he welcomed them all back on board the Mothership. 'You have more than proved yourselves, so now for your final task. Sit down, sit down.'

Dorin carried in another tray of drinks. 'Let's drink to your success, Bright Hearts!'

They sat, curiously awaiting their next assignment. Surely, nothing could be as challenging as the last one…

The Commander took a sip of millienta juice and began: 'You are now going to demonstrate.'

Amelie frowned. 'Demonstrate what exactly?'

'That the Children of Luga renounce war once and for all. A far bigger demonstration than the one you once dreamed of, Amelie. We need you to create a shield around the planet, against the Dark Hearts.'

'Shield?' Tim frowned. 'You mean build one?'

'A Human Shield.' Dorin drew a large circle with his hands. 'An enormous Circle of Peace. And for this you must summon together all the Children of Luga. Sunday the nineteenth of August is the day we have in mind. This is part of a great experiment, one we have never tried on Luga before. You will each need a map of the world.'

'No problem, I've got loads of maps,' Tim said.

Dorin nodded. 'Good. For the next few days then you will sit together in a triangle: one, two, three… Using your maps, you focus on one continent, one country, at a time. Picture clearly every child on the planet coming together and gathering in the centre of their own village or town.'

'Then,' the Commander continued, 'you will raise your hand to greet each one…' He lifted his hand in the Earth Watchers' salute, then touched his heart and bowed low. 'And now send a wave of Peace and Goodwill to each one…' He stopped suddenly. 'Do you have a problem with that, Isla?'

'But surely, that will take forever…'

The Commander shook his head. 'Not at all; you don't realise the power of your mind; and the power of the collective mind is stronger still. One focussed thought of Peace and Goodwill takes seconds. Bring that very thought to every place on your map: plant it, as though it were a seed. Then water it every day with Faith and it will instantly reach the heart of each one, I promise! *You just need to T-R-U-S-T,*' he said emphasising the word. 'You especially, Amelie, need to remember this.'

Amelie blushed, recalling her panic at the Grand Ballroom Sale.

'Your pieces of Lumeanite will help you,' Dorin added. 'Believe, and it will happen! See them turning up in their thousands and millions and the whole event will be all over your social media and television networks in no time!'

Just then they heard a loud squeal and, looking up, watched as a terrifying image appeared on the screen. There, surrounded by flames, was Storm in his little red aircraft…

Chapter Thirty-One

The Dark Hearts Have Struck!

'Sorriel, Thula - we have to go back!' Dorin bellowed, raising the alarm. 'The Dark Hearts have struck…'

'No time to eject the Scoutship,' the Commander said, 'we'll have to go in style. Full throttle, girls – we're on our way!'

Amelie watched the screen in horror. 'But Storm's on fire! He'll die!'

'He has his Stone of Power,' Dorin said evenly. 'It will help to protect him.'

'He'll be terrified all the same. I hope it's not too much for his heart…'

The Commander towered over them and raised his hands, palms facing outwards. 'Remember, Bright Hearts, the power of your minds! Now, do *exactly* as I say…'

A great force hit them, almost knocking them off their feet. 'Hold hands and form a little triangle; that's right, now close your eyes and focus with all your hearts on Storm. Let him know he is safe.'

'We're here!' In no time the great Mothership was hovering over the hangar. Dorin touched a switch on the control panel and a deluge of green plasma-like liquid rained down from its belly and doused the flames. 'We have raised our vibration and yours so no one can see us. Don't worry about the hangar, we'll build that again. All that matters now is Storm!'

They crowded around an opening that had suddenly appeared in the enormous Mothership.

'Take Lara and Freddie and go!'

Beneath them a chute emerged. It was a massive drop; at least the height of a high rise apartment block and ten times more terrifying than the biggest funfair ride they could think of.

'Hurry now, jump down the chute!'

Tim leapt first. He hurled himself out with the girls close behind, clutching Lara and Freddie in their arms. Their bodies now weightless, they flew, as though in a dream! All that mattered now was Storm.

Thick smoke enveloped the spot where the hangar had once stood and Tim, covering his nose and mouth, rushed to Storm's side. 'I'm here,' he choked. 'Please, Storm, don't go…'

But the old man did not respond. He lay in his cockpit, still and pale as a corpse.

Minutes earlier, two figures had appeared at the top of the fields.

'He's in there all right,' one of them said, lifting a pair of binoculars to his eyes. They crossed the field swiftly and took cover under the trees.

'This is where it landed. See? Just behind that shed.' He lingered behind his companion who turned to him with a malicious grin: 'Don't worry, Eli, you big wuss, the cat's not there today.'

'Shut it, Magnus! Think I'm bothered about a ruddy cat?'

Magnus Bottomley-Sligh sniggered, pulled on a balaclava, and began to unscrew a jerry can. 'This'll give him a surprise! He's scared to death of fire…'

'We'll go for the Stone first… then find those tunnels and go halves on whatever's there,' said Eli Dankstone who had absolutely no intention of sharing anything. He leered, picturing the pleasant trip that lay ahead of him: the Bahamas, Seychelles… 'Don't know about you but I'm off on a long cruise!'

Storm had just finished applying a coat of varnish to the wings of his microlight. She'd soon be ready to fly again; one last flight - a little jaunt with young Isla before she left for Washington! Grasping his stick he clambered into the cockpit and closed his eyes; imagined himself cruising pleasantly above the clouds. Lack of sleep and a morning's excitement had left him pleasantly drowsy. A sudden wave of tiredness hit him and in no time at all he had nodded off.

Moments later he awoke with a start. Two balaclava-clad figures stood in the doorway. Instinctively he reached for the little crystal in his pocket. 'What the hell do you pair want?'

Eli Dankstone growled and flicked his cigarette lighter. 'You know what we want! Open your hand and we'll be gone.'

'Clear off!' Storm bellowed but his heart was racing dangerously.

Magnus held up the can and began to pour petrol onto the floor of the hangar, then poised it over the little aircraft. 'We'll see about that,' he crowed.

Eli Dankstone flicked his lighter again, shone the flame in the old man's face.

Storm clutched his chest. The smell of petrol was making him feel distinctly queasy but with a sudden surge of power he grabbed his stick and struck out at Eli Dankstone who slipped and fell. A burst of flames leapt from the ground, roaring and crackling like a hungry beast. Thick black smoke swallowed up the air and panicking, Eli and Magnus retreated.

The world went black and Storm felt himself falling. His parachute billowed above him and he drifted down, slowly, silently, and landed safely in a soft, grassy field. He saw a huge tunnel emerging from the sky, a tunnel of light. Then he heard Dorin's voice in the distance: *All that matters is Storm!*

The flames had subsided now and the hangar dripped with a plasma-like gel. 'I am dead,' he murmured and a great peace came over him. His fear of fire had died with him.

Meanwhile, Eli and Magnus looked around them, mystified. The flames had disappeared along with the shed, leaving only a cloud of black smoke and some sticky green gel. All at once Eli uttered a wail of horror. *Help me!* His feet left the ground and he soared upwards, as though propelled by some unseen force, and finally disappeared into the clouds.

'I'll check his pulse,' Tim said calmly, taking the old man's hand in his own.

'He feels very clammy,' Amelie murmured, stroking his brow.

'Storm Trott, don't you dare!' Isla commanded. 'We still have to get this machine off the ground, remember?'

They waited, hardly daring to breathe.

'Look,' Tim whispered.

Storm twitched a little as though waking from a dream. Very slowly, colour returned to his cheeks. 'Will someone please pinch me, and check I'm still here? I saw a tunnel of light and thought I was ...'

'Dead? We thought you were too,' Isla said softly. 'Are you really all right?'

'Don't fuss, girl!' he blustered, sitting bolt upright. 'Just a bit scorched around the whiskers but otherwise tickety-boo. Thank heavens for that flame retardant varnish!'

Isla squeezed his hand. 'We concentrated ever so hard on you being safe and alive.'

'Looks like it worked, my dears. You and the Earth

Watchers have saved my life.'

Isla planted a kiss on his cheek. 'Oh Storm, I do love you! Why don't I phone my dad and get him to check you over?'

'Isla, I told you, don't fuss! Now, what happened to that pair of damned rogues?'

'Magnus ran off like he'd seen a ghost!'

'And Eli's off on the trip of his life,' Tim laughed, helping the old man out of the cockpit. 'That tunnel you saw was the chute we came down. We landed, and Eli took off!'

'Sucked right up into the Mothership,' Amelie said, handing Storm his stick. 'I wonder what'll happen next?'

'What next?' Tim stared at them, stony-faced. 'This one's for the police.' He reached for his mobile phone. 'I'm phoning them right now.'

Chapter Thirty-Two
The Underground Tunnels

'Well, well, Elias Dankstone! We've been trying to nab him for years.' Sergeant Buggeley opened his incident book and began to take notes. 'Any witnesses?' he asked hopefully.

'Just us three,' Tim said. Plus a cat and a dog and four extra-terrestrial friends, but he thought he'd better leave that bit out. Also the fact that Eli Dankstone was probably several million miles away by now, heading for the outer reaches of the solar system...

Despite interviews with neighbours and an early morning raid the following day, the police made no further progress with their enquiries. As for poor Magnus, he'd been in bed all day according to his mother, struck down with some dreadful virus. And in fact, when Magnus Bottomley-Sligh did arrive back home he didn't look too well at all.

'Whatever is it, Nussy darling?' Mona Bottomley-Sligh fussed.

A frenzied Magnus threw himself down on the sofa. 'It's Eli!' he sobbed. 'He's been abducted by aliens!'

Maynard looked up and assumed an unusually sympathetic tone. 'Oh dear, how dreadful...' Then he turned sharply. 'Little green men - what are you blathering on about, you dozy great lump?'

'Don't call him that, Maynard!' Mona admonished.

Magnus continued to bawl. 'Sucked up into the clouds…'

'Have you totally lost your mind? Mona! Do something, will you? Cake, anything to stuff in his stupid face…'

Mona hovered, attempting to cajole her son with Chocolate Hob Nobs and Custard Creams. Then she remembered a pack of cream doughnuts at the back of the fridge. 'Here, sweetie, these will calm you down…'

But even doughnuts failed to pacify Magnus and he continued to shed hot tears of regret, not for his accomplice but for yet another great opportunity lost.

Later that day Lucy returned from London in good spirits. However, it wasn't long before she caught sight of the wreckage at the far end of the garden. 'Honestly, Storm, what are you like? I go away for a couple of days and come back to this, a burned down shed!' She made a sweeping gesture towards the pile of rubble in its place. 'At least you and your microlight are in one piece, I suppose…'

Storm lowered his eyes, like a naughty child caught out.

'How could you be so careless?'

'Don't shout at him, Mum,' Amelie said firmly. 'He's still a bit wobbly - he's had an *astroshus* shock.'

'Atrocious shock?'

'Yes, Eli Dankstone and Magnus. Don't worry though, Sergeant Buggeley's on it.'

'That's terrible!' Lucy looked Amelie up and down curiously. 'Amelie, you seem different, love - in a good way, I mean.'

'Oh, yes, I'm fine, we all are; everything's fine. You look different too, Mum - at least ten years younger. So, come on then, tell us about your trip.'

'I've been longing to tell you all!' Lucy grinned, her cheeks flushed with excitement. 'I've got ten new commissions…' and she rattled off a list of famous names they'd mostly never heard of. But some they had: a well-known footballer, a TV presenter, and even a member of the Royal Family.

'Also someone who wants to remain anonymous...' She tapped the side of her nose.

'But who, Mum, who?' Amelie begged. 'I'll lend you my autograph book, if you like.'

'Top secret for now,' Lucy teased. 'And it's the first sitting tomorrow so I need you all out of the house for a couple of hours.'

Never mind, thought Amelie. We have our secrets too...

'Are you really ok, Storm?' Lucy called over her shoulder, already halfway down the path.

'Stop fussing!' Storm growled.

They all followed her back to the house, knowing that soon they would have to tell her everything; but perhaps not quite yet.

'Timing is important,' Isla agreed. 'But we've got lots to tell you, Storm.'

The old man frowned, trying to take it all in. 'Yes, my two young Earth Watchers,' he said finally, addressing Amelie and Tim, 'it's all falling into place at last... but there's still one more piece to this jigsaw puzzle.' He looked directly at Amelie. 'You remember I told you how very like Eggy you are?'

Amelie nodded. 'Oh yes, and you said, "Even though"...'

'Well, the thing is this: Michael was *Joan's* son not Ted's; she had him already when they first met.'

'Which means then,' Tim said, looking shaken, 'we're not actually related to *you*...'

'That's awful,' said Amelie. 'I don't know who I am anymore.' *Never forget who you are*, the Commander had said, but for her beloved Storm not to be their great-grandfather anymore, that was just too much to bear.

'But of course we're related, Tim, just not by blood. And loved all the more for it! You see, Joan is clearly an Earth Watcher too...'

Tim looked like he was about to fall over. 'So, maybe this

means we're even more Earth Watcher than we thought!'

'I suppose you are.' He beckoned them into his study. 'Now, look what's in here…'

And sure enough, there was Michael's little figure of Yoda, still in the roll-top desk, exactly as he had promised. Things really could be in two places at once, it seemed…

And then another surprising thing happened. Three days later, a beautiful new hangar appeared, just as Dorin had promised. Far nicer than the old one, they all agreed. It was bright and airy with shelves for all of Storm's tools. There was even a shiny new floor with a trap door that led to the underground tunnels. But how would they possibly tell their mother the truth: that the Earth Watchers had come in the night and re-built it?

'A couple of old friends knocked it up?' Tim suggested. He had managed to prise open the trap door and was shining his torch into the damp blackness below. 'Coming? Isla, you hold this while I go down first. Then you two can follow. And mind your heads!' he warned.

Once down there, they crept forward slowly, examining the walls for any signs the Earth Watchers may have left. 'Imagine, no one's been down here for seventy years or so…'

'It smells like it,' Amelie said and sneezed.

There was one main passage which led they imagined to the house, with a network of smaller passages branching off on both sides.

'Look over here!' Isla called. She shone the torch into a little recess, illuminating a huge casket, encrusted with rose coloured stones. 'These are pieces of Shamalite, I'm pretty sure. I wonder how Larry and the White House dogs are doing…'

'That reminds me, I guess we should get back to our maps,' Tim said. 'We haven't much time left before the Human Shield.'

'Just one quick peep, please…?' Isla reached into the

casket and lifted out a couple of old books, inscribed with strange symbols. 'These are priceless – artifacts of extra-terrestrial life!'

There were lots of little drawings in there too: buildings, trees, even a winged horse. 'And a hovercraft just like the ones we saw on Zalnea...'

Amelie found a tiny house with miniature people inside, all seated around a table. 'Do you think one day everyone will accept there's intelligent life on other planets?'

Tim looked doubtful. 'Maybe once we have intelligent life on our own...'

On their way back to the house they looked in on the garden studio and noticed an easel set up with a new canvas.

'Looks like Mum's forgotten and left it uncovered,' Tim observed. 'It's meant to be a secret. Hey, that looks a lot like...'

'It is, it's *him!*' Amelie clamped a hand over her mouth. 'That means he's been here and we missed him. I wonder if he remembers signing my autograph book?'

Tim rolled his eyes. 'It'll be Mickey Mouse next.'

The two girls ignored him.

'Awesome,' Isla laughed. 'He's my mom's favourite singer too.'

'Hey,' Amelie nudged Tim. 'Do you think he's married?'

'Mickey Mouse?'

'No, silly!'

'You know he is,' Tim said impatiently. 'You've seen his wife on the telly. Come on now, maps!'

'Ah, well...' Amelie murmured, lingering a moment longer. 'There's still Lawrence, I suppose...'

Chapter Thirty-Three

Storm and Isla Take a Spin

Two days later in Downing Street the Prime Minister came down to breakfast looking rather dishevelled.

'Oh dear, bad night, Prime Minister?' a parliamentary aide enquired, offering a pot of strong coffee.

'Thank you, Hobbleton. Yes, I'm afraid that naughty Larry kept me awake, insisted on sleeping on my head. Oh, good Lord, that can't be the time! Put a video call through to the White House, will you? I must speak urgently to the President.'

'But it's three in the morning in Washington, Prime Minister…'

'No matter, Hobbleton, the President's a night owl like me.'

The President was, in fact, about to take a stroll in the White House grounds with the dogs.

'Hey, Prime Minister, you ok? Looking a bit rough today! Just saying…'

'We must talk,' the voice at the other end bellowed. 'Urgently, regarding the missile launches next Monday…'

'All set to go, locked and loaded! Hey, down boy! Sit!' The two small dogs had begun to yap uncontrollably.

The Prime Minister sighed impatiently. 'Yes, yes, I've read your tweets. *Without them we're vulnerable to attack, both here and further afield…'*

'Sure, the threat from Outer Space is extremely disturbing; we've had a good deal of UFO activity here lately - one sniffing around over the White House.'

'Here too, over St. James's Park.' The Prime Minister took a quick gulp of coffee. 'But I can't help wondering, supposing they're actually here to help? And what if we risk blowing ourselves up in the process?'

A further chorus of barking interrupted their conversation. 'They've been like this for days,' the President said irritably. 'One thing though; whatever you say, I don't intend to back down now, Prime Minister. Down, you crazy mutt, down! One or two launches won't be the end of the world…'

'Are you sure about that?' the Prime Minister muttered sourly over the noise, hoping the President governed the nation rather better than that pair of over-excited White House dogs.

When the day of Isla's departure finally arrived they all found themselves far too occupied with their maps to be sad. The little playhouse now served as their Operations Room with a *Do Not Disturb* notice on the door and a triangle of chairs inside. 'We mustn't forget the Earth Watchers' salute,' Tim said, following the Commander's instructions precisely.

It was Isla's bright idea to employ their Stones of Power. 'Let's try holding them over one country at a time.'

Amelie proposed they all join hands for a while and imagine a big three-dimensional screen where they would watch it all happening. 'A good exercise in mind-wandering,' she said. 'We'll visualise them arriving in their thousands!'

'Millions,' Tim added. And they all agreed. It was exactly like that moment in the Mothership when they helped to save Storm.

'So, now Storm's recovered,' Tim proposed at the end of their final session, 'I think we should tell him our plans.'

They found him in his bright new hangar, admiring his

little red aircraft. 'Ready now for her next flight,' he said with a satisfied grin. He had carefully repainted the wings and was buffing them up with a cloth.

'Very nice, but what are those shiny things you've stuck on the wings?' Amelie enquired.

'Solar panels, of course,' Storm replied. 'So I don't need fuel. However, that won't be for another few months.'

'Awesome!' said Isla. 'Great for cutting carbon emissions.'

'It was Dorin's idea. Hopefully I'll have it up and flying by the next time you come. That's if we're all still here,' he murmured bleakly.

'Storm, we have some more news for you...' Amelie shifted from one foot to the other and glanced at the others for help. 'Lawrence is taking me and Tim to London tomorrow and he's treating us to dinner and Mum was hoping to come too but she's working, which is just as well because...'

'Spit it out, girl!'

'We're creating a Human Shield...'

'A human *what?*'

Between them they pieced together their latest story: their flying visits (literally, Amelie added) to Downing Street and the White House and their forthcoming plan to halt the missile launches.

'We were like, really - *what us?*' said Isla, still wondering if she was about to awaken from a dream. 'Change the minds of world leaders? You gotta be kidding!'

'The biggest Call for Peace in human history,' Tim said, speaking words that were not his own. 'But if that doesn't work...'

'Yes,' Storm grunted, 'it doesn't bear thinking about. But, Good Lord, this shouldn't be all down to you, a bunch of young kids. We adults have let you down badly. Luga? We're no more than some *Ludicrously Unfortunate Galactic Accident...*' He continued to buff up the paintwork then handed Amelie the cloth. 'Here, a bit more spit and polish

197

and you'll soon see your face in it.'

Amelie rubbed away at the wing but her mind was elsewhere. How things had changed since their last day at school. And how she had changed too! 'I wish you could join us tomorrow, Storm,' she said, looking up at him wistfully. 'You're like an honorary child, after all.'

The old man scratched his head and chuckled. 'Well, that's the nicest compliment I've had in ninety-four years. But don't you worry - you'll have Lawrence there to help, after all.'

'But that's part of the problem,' Tim said. 'How *do* we explain all this to him?'

'I suspect Lawrence understands more than you give him credit for. But I'll have a word with him tonight if you like.'

'Would you really?' Amelie was halfway between laughter and tears. The reality of the Human Shield had suddenly hit her. 'And then there's Mum, of course. She'll go crazy when she finds out, and she doesn't even know about our meeting Dad - yet. Will you make absolutely sure she's not worried about us?'

Storm put an arm around her. 'Leave it with me, Amelie. I'll think of something. We can't keep all this from her much longer.'

Amelie nodded. 'It's a bit scary though, what if no one turns up?' She bit her lip, wishing she hadn't said that. That was the old Amelie. *Never forget who you are!* 'Anyway, she said quickly, 'we've done everything we possibly could so even if no one turns up, we'll be there; lone protesters if necessary.'

'Just what I was thinking,' Isla said. 'I'll do it on my own gladly. By the way…' She stooped down to unzip her travel bag. 'I've made something for you.' She unfolded what looked like a large flag and handed it to Tim.

'*Children in Charge!* Isla, that's brilliant, just what we need!'

'Banners,' said Amelie. 'Why didn't we think of them before?'

'Because we were all too focussed on our maps... Anyway, there's plenty more here so take as many as you like. A little thank you for the most amazing summer of my life.' She stopped suddenly to glance at her watch. 'Hey, Grandpa Storm, I've really only come to say goodbye to you, and return your manual.' She planted a kiss on the old man's cheek. 'Not that we do goodbyes anymore...' She paused, swallowing her tears. 'I'm flying back tonight and like Amelie I'm excited and nervous all in one.'

'You'll be awesome, girl!' Storm replied in a terrible American accent. They all laughed and their nervousness disappeared, for now at least. 'Talking of flying, why don't we take a little spin right now, just you and me, Isla? Not far, just the stars and back. Hop in.'

Isla threw her arms around her old friend. 'I'm going to miss you so much, Grandpa Storm,' she said, privately wondering how she would ever bear to lose him when the time came. 'Come on then, Captain...' and bravely, but not without trepidation, she climbed up into the cockpit next to him.

Tim flung open the back door of the hangar and the little microlight taxied along the somewhat uneven runway. They picked up speed and very soon Isla and the old man were in the air, cruising above the trees. Then something went dreadfully wrong and they were obliged to make a very bumpy emergency landing.

'That's it,' Storm said dejectedly, 'my very last flight!'

'Rubbish!' Isla said. 'It's not the end of the world.' Then she laughed. 'I really shouldn't say that, should I? Here, give me the manual a moment. Let's have a look and see if we can fix it.' She consulted the index and flicked through the pages. 'Spark plugs, I reckon,' she said, and reached into the tool box for a spanner. She set to work and, after a few minutes, put it down with an ear-to-ear grin. 'There, sorted. Except you won't need spark plugs once you go solar-powered!'

They thought the long, hot summer would never end but just as they left the hangar, dark clouds appeared overhead and the first few drops of rain began to fall.

'Oh no, not now!' Amelie gasped, visibly flustered. 'It hasn't rained for weeks.' And as she spoke, the heavens opened and they ran for cover in the playhouse. They huddled together, waiting for the storm to pass.

'It's only a drop of rain,' Tim said, watching the torrential downpour outside.

Amelie shook her head. No one will come, the sly Voice of Doubt insisted, but she resolutely ignored it. 'Okay, Isla's dad will be here soon to take her to the airport. Why don't we all just…?' She was about to say "send a wave of Peace and Goodwill" when a faint sound of wind chimes echoed outside the playhouse.

'It's him,' Tim whispered, cocking his ear. A loud clap of thunder followed and they listened, enthralled, as the Commander began to sing:

And still the rain is falling
For all the world to see
But now I know…
Peace Begins With Me.

'What a beautiful song,' Amelie breathed. Whatever might happen next, the Earth Watchers had it all under control…

The Commander's voice continued: *Very soon, when the Cosmic Clock strikes, I shall depart for I am needed elsewhere.* And with this he appeared before them in a burst of light and raised his long-fingered hand: *Tomorrow is a new story already in the making…Yes, Tim, the biggest Call for Peace in human history…*

Chapter Thirty-Four

Saving Luga

In Southern Africa the sun rose over Kgale Hill and Baboloki Mosi awoke from his dreams. *'Dumela! Dumela!'* He pulled the covers over his head but the voices outside were insistent: *'Baboloki, dumela!'* Wearily, he climbed out of bed and peered out through the open window. There, waiting in the street below were at least a hundred children, shaking leg rattles and banging drums: 'Come quickly!'

Five thousand miles away in the little Dutch town of Edam, Lotte and Lars watched in wonder as hordes of children thronged the old cobbled streets. *'Kom snel,'* one of them beckoned as they headed towards the Raadhuis.

But in Tokyo it was already evening and twins Hana and Genzo had just received a call from their cousin, Akimasa. *'Hayaku kite!'* he said, sounding very excited: *'Can you get here fast? There's some kind of festival going on...'*

Meanwhile, in London the rain was still falling:

'It's Sunday the nineteenth of August, and this is Vanessa Scoop in the studio…

Breaking News! Reports are now coming in of thousands upon thousands of children, assembling all over the world. Here's our World Affairs correspondent, Jeremy Loudly, in Central London. Jeremy, can you talk us through what's happening right now…?'

'Yes, Vanessa, despite heavy rain, they've been descending on Central London all morning. All over the city traffic has been forced to a standstill. It's all extremely well organised, I have to say; no incidents at all. Quite a few *Children in Charge* banners, but NO ADULTS, that's the extraordinary thing! Oh, apart from one… Good Lord - it's publisher and art critic Lawrence Goodman! I'll see if I can get him to talk to us later…'

'Children in charge – in charge of what exactly? Are they about to make some demands, do you think? Cut school hours perhaps? More holidays for five to sixteen year olds? A bid for state-funded pocket money in line with the cost of living…?'

'As to why they're here seems very unclear…'

'Extraordinary! Look, Jeremy, over there in Parliament Square; just by the statue of Gandhi. A young girl with a cat on a lead; and a boy with a dog, giving out banners…'

'Yes, Vanessa. Mahatma Gandhi, Man of Peace, and look, now they're being joined by…'

'… Ah, it's James Bowen and his famous Street Cat Called Bob! I recognised Bob by the scarf. Yes, I interviewed them on the Breakfast Show just before their film was released. Jeremy, I'm sorry, we have to leave you there and continue with the rest of today's news, but we'll return to you later for any further developments.'

'And now, we go back to our special report on the Children in Charge March. We've since had reports coming in from Geneva, and New York. Yes, and Darjeeling and Tokyo. Wait, here's some more: from South America, China, Russia, New Zealand, Australia, even remote villages in Africa. Jeremy, what's happening now in London? Have we heard anything from Downing Street yet?'

'Good afternoon, Vanessa. Yes, indeed. The Prime Minister has just appeared outside Number Ten, with Larry, the Downing Street cat. They appear to be walking towards the crowds right now. One or two more adults have joined the group too. Taxi drivers, policeman, men and women; tourists from all over the world are taking part. The strange thing is, it's all uncannily quiet, and *everyone* is smiling.'

Undeterred by the rain, one hundred thousand and fifty-seven children, one dog and three cats (Freddie, Bob, and Larry) began to form a shield around Central London, and as the shield grew larger, still more of them came.

'*No one will come!*' Tim whimpered in a voice very like Amelie's.

Amelie grinned good-naturedly and stooped to pick up Freddie. 'I can't believe it, you know, Tim; there's more than I ever imagined! I'm glad you're here too, Lawrence…' She looked up at him and her heart glowed like Dorin's.

Lawrence Goodman squeezed her arm. 'I wouldn't have missed it for the world! Though, to be honest, I've no idea how you made all this happen. Have you seen all those TV crews? By the way, I've just been taking a few videos too. I'm setting you up with your own YouTube channel…' He stopped abruptly, aware of his own voice. A silent London was, literally, unheard of yet today it was all so still and peaceful, apart from the pleasant chatter of goldfinches and robins on the far side of the square.

A sense of expectancy hung over them all, as though everyone was waiting for someone very important to arrive.

'Time has stood still,' Jeremy Loudly said quietly.

The long silence was broken as police helicopters hovered overhead and suddenly the broadcast was interrupted and television screens everywhere went blank. The rain had stopped now and sunshine was beginning to break through the clouds.

'Happy now, Amelie?' said Lawrence Goodman with a smile. 'What a wonderful day it's turned out to be!'

'I think I know what my next book will be,' she whispered as a beam of sunlight struck her poppy-red hair.

Lawrence laughed. 'I rather think I do too, Amelie. This is a day to go down in history. Oh, good heavens, what's that?' He gasped as scores of bright lights appeared in the sky. 'Just look at that! Some flypast that is, eh Tim?'

'Lawrence, it's the Earth Watchers!' Tim said. 'And all this will be happening across the whole world, just like they promised. If only Isla and Storm were here…'

'Wait!' Lawrence shielded his eyes. 'Look up there!'

Following the Earth Watchers was a small aircraft. It was flying quite low, low enough for them to see its solar panels flashing in the sunlight, and a pilot wearing old RAF goggles. He had a passenger with him, waving a scarf jubilantly.

'Storm! He must have been planning this all along!' Tim laughed, waving with both arms. 'And look who's with him…'

'Mum!' For the second time that summer Amelie was weightless, literally walking on air! So happy, she was swept off her feet and found herself perched on Lawrence's shoulders. Glancing down she was met with a look of surprise.

'How on earth did you get up there?' Lawrence laughed. 'You certainly stand out from the crowd!'

'I'm sorry, Lawrence, I haven't a clue, unless…' It dawned on her suddenly: Yes, of course, she had Earth Watchers' blood! Being different didn't seem such a bad thing after all.

'This means,' Tim said, watching the little microlight circling above them, 'it's not the End of the World after all.'

'No,' Lawrence agreed, just as someone thrust a microphone into his face, 'I rather think it's the beginning of a new and better one!'

'Lawrence Goodman, so perhaps you can explain what's going on here,' said the man with the microphone.

'Actually, Jeremy, I think the people you need to speak to are right here with me.' He handed the microphone up to Amelie. 'Go on, Amelie, your call…'

'Wait a moment,' Jeremy Loudly spluttered, 'I have some questions for you…'

But, still balanced on Lawrence's shoulders, Amelie began to address the waiting crowds.

'You may be wondering why you've all come here today…' And, as her voice rang out over the hub-bub, silence fell once more. 'Amazingly, you heard our call; the greatest Call for Peace in human history. Our planet is in great danger.' She paused and a pin could be heard to drop in Parliament Square. 'You see, the adults of the world can no longer be trusted. You are the ones to take charge of her safety now, and therefore our own. War is no longer an option. If we are ever to reach our twenties we have to rid the world of ALL weapons of destruction right NOW. Tomorrow is too late! Are you ready? Will you help us?'

'Yes!' cried a lone voice from the crowd, 'No more war! Children in Charge!' and soon, thousands more took up the chant: *No more war! Children in Charge!*

This is all so easy, thought Amelie with delight. They are speaking through me!

'As you have just seen, we are not alone.' She pointed up at the sky where a huge double rainbow had appeared. 'The Earth Watchers are here which means there is Hope for us all! Be warned though because many will try to convince you they are to be feared. But *we* know this isn't true, and we can prove it! The Earth Watchers are our friends…'

Suddenly, she had landed on her feet again and everyone was gathering round, hugging her and begging for selfies.

'Well, we apologise for that earlier interruption to our service but we can now return you to Jeremy Loudly, live in Central London. Jeremy, you are with Amelie Joan Trott, I believe, co-organiser of the worldwide *Children in Charge March?*'

'That's right, Vanessa,' said Jeremy Loudly, still mystified by Amelie's extraordinary address. 'Let's just move somewhere a little quieter, shall we…?' A cameraman joined him and hustled them all through the jostling crowd towards the south side of Parliament Square. 'Yes, here will do nicely.'

#

'Well, thank you for joining us, Amelie and Timothy Trott. Would you tell us, please, the background to today's remarkable international event?'

'Me and Tim…,' Amelie began then stopped abruptly. 'Shall I start again?'

'We're live,' hissed Jeremy Loudly. 'Nothing wrong, do carry on. We're very interested to hear your story.'

'Well, Tim and me, and our best friend Isla Batty from Washington…'

'Let's see if we can get a link to Washington… Vanessa? Yes, yes, good, good! We now have Isla Batty too, live from Washington DC…'

Between them they told their story: how Amelie had first come to meet the Earth Watchers; their trips in the Scoutship, their first Solar Cruise. Isla in Washington spoke of the little balls of light that had taken so many people in Havenbridge by surprise and finally, Tim explained the Earth Watchers' deep concern for our planet and the deadly weapons that are now threatening its survival. 'Why are we here? Today, we children demand an end to war. We are not taking no for an answer…'

It was then that Amelie recalled Sorriel's words: *One day you'll tell the world about us… and this will be sooner than you think!*

Jeremy Loudly said nothing. Instead, he stared into space with a rapturous expression on his face. These guys really were quite something!

Someone back in the studio shouted into his earphones. 'Get the show moving, Jez! We're running out of time…'

Chapter Thirty-Five

The World Has Gone Barking Mad

The little carriage clock on Ernestine Snarkey's mantelpiece was about to strike six. She disappeared into her kitchen, just as she did each evening at precisely this time. Having made a pot of tea, she placed two Rich Tea biscuits on a plate, and returned to switch on the television set in the corner. At this point her face blanched and she grasped the arm of her chair to steady herself. 'It can't be...'

There in the centre of the screen was a girl, bearing a striking resemblance to Amelie Trott! She appeared to be leading a tribe of unruly children through the streets of London but the trouble was Ernestine was forced to admit, they were not actually unruly at all. On the contrary, they were as orderly as soldiers on parade. Then a terrible thought crossed her mind. Was this what the Specks had meant, a protest against *her*?

'Children in charge? Aliens? The world has gone barking mad!' She gasped in disbelief. There she was with World Affairs correspondent, Jeremy Loudly.

She rose and pressed her nose close to the screen. 'A flaming publishing contract, you're telling me?' she screeched in Jeremy Loudly's face. 'She can't even spell!'

\#

Good as his word, Lawrence Goodman treated them all

to dinner, though it was not quite the sumptuous repast he'd planned. Because of all the TV interviews and journalists popping up wherever they went, they had caught the late train back to Havenbridge, where Lucy and Storm (still wearing his old flying helmet) were waiting with an enormous bag of chips from the Chinese Takeaway in Littlehaven, five Magnums, and a giant box of Maltesers to follow.

'My treat!' Lawrence said with such a beautiful smile that Amelie felt her heart leap with gratitude. 'Just a pity we have no bubbly to toast our young heroes.'

'What an amazing day!' Lucy kicked off her shoes and sank down on the sofa. 'Lawrence...' She touched his arm gently and smiled. 'Thank you for looking after the children so wonderfully today.'

Lawrence placed his hand over hers and left it there just long enough for Amelie to notice. 'My pleasure,' he replied with another lovely smile and Lucy's face turned just a tiny bit pink. 'Tim love,' she said hurriedly, 'switch on the telly, will you? Let's see if we can catch some news.'

'Turn it up a bit, will you?' said Storm. 'Oh, my goodness, look at you two with Jeremy Loudly! Can't stand the man but never mind...'

'He's nice,' Amelie remonstrated. 'Don't be so judgmental, Storm.'

The old man roared with laughter. Young Amelie really had blossomed these past few weeks. 'Well done! It's all been the making of you, my dear!'

Lucy watched them in disbelief. Her two adorable children, taking on the world with a force she'd never witnessed before. It was all too much... 'And look, there's our lovely Isla in Washington!' She brushed a stray tear from her cheek, and shot a disapproving look at Storm. 'But don't think I've forgiven you yet! Tricking me like that...'

Storm grinned. 'It's all I could think of, to show you first hand. Let's face it, Lucy; you'd have never believed me otherwise.'

That morning, Storm had lured Lucy into the microlight while he taxied onto the runway. 'Just to balance the weight,' he explained, ignoring her protests (*No, Storm, you know I have work to do!*). But this was urgent too, he'd insisted, and would only require a moment of her time. (*Well, he reasoned, a moment is subjective, after all.*) The next thing she knew, they were flying over rooftops and heading for London with Storm bawling over the deafening noise of the engine: 'You'll thank me for this for the rest of your life…'

And very soon she found herself smiling. Thanks to Storm she had witnessed, first hand, a flypast of UFOs and more than one hundred thousand and fifty-seven children, one dog and three cats, all gathered in Parliament Square. After that, nothing seemed impossible anymore. Not even Michael living on some far distant planet. Or the ten foot tall man she'd been seeing for weeks.

All the day's excitement had now given way to a wave of exhaustion, and Amelie's eyes were beginning to close. Freddie and Lara had curled up contentedly beside her, twitching in their sleep and dreaming of London, the crowds, and the noise.

'Bed now!' Lucy ordered. 'You too, Tim – remember, you have a Press Conference tomorrow.'

'Wait!' Tim said, groping in the cushions for the remote control. 'Jeremy's back…'

'Not looking good, I'm afraid,' Storm said sadly, as a group of stony faced men and women appeared on the screen. 'Blasted warmongering fools, whenever will they see sense?'

'…Breaking News!' announced Jeremy Loudly. 'With tensions growing around the world and just hours to go before the biggest missile launches the world has ever known, World Leaders have gathered in Geneva, following today's extraordinary international protests. After several hours of heated discussion it seems they have, at last, reached a unanimous decision...'

The room fell silent as the world held its breath.

'...Pressure from young people around the world has resulted in a universal and unprecedented change of heart...'

At which point the stony faced leaders broke into smiles and exchanged handshakes while Tim jumped up and down and cheered as though his favourite football team had just scored a winning goal. 'You know what this means then, Amelie?' he said. 'The Commander will be...'

'...over the moon?'

They clutched each other, crying with laughter at their own stupid joke.

So, of course, there was now very little left to explain.

For Andrew Batty and Bettina Rivas it was the unexpected consequences of the Human Shield that reassured them. There was at last the promise of Peace on Earth. 'This is a great start, at least,' Bettina said. And as for their daughter insisting she'd flown a spacecraft? Well, they reminded themselves; when had she ever been known to lie...?

Chapter Thirty-Six
The Cosmic Clock

In mid-October, Isla returned unexpectedly to Havenbridge. Her mother had been called to an international conference in London which happily coincided with their half-term break.

It was just then that Dorin appeared too, tapping at the playhouse window one day, just as he had done once before.

Amelie looked up from her work. 'Dorin!' How wonderful it was to hear his funny, robotic voice once more!

He placed a hand on his heart and bowed low and at once his voice changed. 'You've really grown up, haven't you...?' he said, looking her up and down.

'I hope not,' she laughed. 'Even though I'm getting quite old – I'm eleven now, you know.'

'And quite the celebrity, it seems!'

Amelie blushed. 'I don't know about that. But the funny thing is, since being on the telly and stuff everyone wants to be my friend. I only had Isla and Storm before. And you.' She grinned. 'Even Miss Snarkey pretends to like me now. She even agreed to have me back! Anyway, you must have known Isla was here. She's with Tim. Shall we go and find them?'

They strolled off together and found Tim and Isla kicking a football around at the back of the house.

'You must see my railway,' Tim said at once. 'I'm installing a runway for flying trains, once I've figured out how to get them off the ground – and there's a Space Port too.'

Dorin hissed like a steam iron. 'One we'll use many times in the future, I'm sure.'

'And I've got some news for you all too,' Isla said, smiling mysteriously, 'though I'm not allowed to tell you just yet.'

Reading her thoughts, Dorin smiled knowingly then he glanced around as though searching for someone else. 'Now where's my old friend Storm?'

'Where do you think?' Tim gestured towards the fields. 'In his new hangar with Thomas.'

'Thomas and Libby Lambe live with us now,' Amelie said excitedly. 'Thomas helps Storm with the garden and Libby looks after the house. She makes the best custard and chips ever…'

Dorin screwed up his face. 'Strange things you Lugans eat.'

Isla giggled. 'Libby Lambe, what an awesome name!'

Dorin began to hiss like a steam iron again. 'No more from the Dark Hearts then?'

It turned out that Eli Dankstone had been shipped off to Daktron. 'A cold and dark planet, about as far from the sun as you can get. Peopled with selfish, cruel types just like himself. And there he'll stay until further notice…'

'Well, please don't bring him back here again,' Amelie pleaded, taking his arm. 'Now you're here, you must come and meet Mum and Auntie Bettina.'

Dorin shook his head. 'Another time, Amelie; the Cosmic Clock is ticking so I have to get back before it strikes.'

Cosmic Clock - how would that work, Tim wondered, since there's only NOW?

They had forgotten how easily Dorin could read their thoughts. 'I speak symbolically, Tim; it's not so much a clock as a cycle of experience. The Commander is about to undergo a Great Transformation. He'll be wiser and mightier than ever before.'

They could think of nothing more to say. *Awesome* didn't seem quite enough.

'I know, let's have a photo to show them at least,' Isla said, angling her mobile phone to fit them all in. 'A group selfie!' It would be something to see her through the long winter months before she returned to Havenbridge once more.

The three children gathered around Dorin and put on their best smiles.

'Perfect!' Isla beamed. 'Look, these are good ones of us all! Let's go show our moms while Dorin's with Storm.'

In the studio Lucy was about to reveal the portrait she had painted for Isla's Christmas present. Hearing voices outside, she glanced up and smiled. 'I was going to call you all in for your tea!'

'We've just taken some photos of Dorin!' Amelie said. 'Show them, Isla…'

Intrigued, Lucy and Bettina peered at the little screen.

'Unfortunately, there seems to be only the three of you here,' Bettina said.

Puzzled, Isla snatched back her phone and took another look. There it was: a perfectly clear image of herself with Tim and Amelie; and a big bright light where Dorin had stood.

#

'I'll tell you my news later,' Isla said after supper the next evening. She paused, delighting in keeping the suspense going a little longer.

'No, tell us now!'

'Well…' she teased, her solemn face betraying none of the excitement she felt. 'I'm sorry this may be a shock for you both but…'

'Just tell us!'

'It seems like we'll be seeing a lot more of one another next year. Mom's got a new job and we're coming back to live in London!'

Even before she'd finished, Amelie had leapt to her feet. 'Oh Isla, that's the best news ever, isn't it, Tim?'

'Oh,' Tim said glumly, 'is that all?' and Isla punched his arm. 'Hey, that hurt, you great half-American bully!'

They all laughed but stopped abruptly as a familiar tapping sound came from upstairs.

'Eggy!' Tim said, surprised. 'We haven't heard from her for months.'

Amelie nodded. 'Maybe because she's at peace, her mission accomplished.'

'You think?' said Isla. 'Anyway, let's go see what she wants…'

Tap, tap, tap… Curiously, they followed; climbed the stairs to the stained glass window where they all paused to salute the Commander, then on to the Ballroom where three months ago their fortune had miraculously changed. They continued up the last flight of stairs and, just as they were about to set foot in the attic, the tapping ceased.

Isla gazed around her in awe. Amelie had set up another little desk by the window, complete with a lamp, transonometer, and her lucky rainbow pen; and there on a gigantic platform that took up most of the room was Tim's ever growing railway. 'It'll soon be bigger than the real Havenbridge Junction,' she gasped, taking in the vast array of scenery and crowded platforms, and the busy roadways beyond the station itself. 'That is *so* cool, Tim!'

'See the Space Port?' Tim placed a little silver-clad figure with conker-brown skin next to one of the Scoutships. 'This one is you.'

'Tim, you're awesome,' Isla laughed and was about to give Tim a big hug when Amelie seized her arm.

'Isla, look over there!'

They all stopped what they were doing and gathered around the big attic window. There, in a fiery blaze of light, stood the Commander. He towered above them and smiled, raising his hand in the Earth Watchers' salute. They stared in astonishment as his noble face transformed: becoming first a child, then a young woman; one face after another, each one fading into the next. Lifetimes of faces appeared, all past and future versions of himself throughout eternity.

Until the next time, he said, which may be sooner than you think. It is now down to you, Children of Luga…

Bowing deeply, he raised his long-fingered hand once more and they heard a distant sound, gong-like.

'It's the Cosmic Clock,' Tim murmured. And, sure enough, it struck as predicted, and the Commander dissolved into the Light once more. But they could still hear his voice, as clearly as though he were there. *I'll be back, Bright Hearts; you have much still to do!*

And anyone glancing up at Cloud Hill that night might have seen, just to the right of the gibbous moon, a streak of light flash across the sky.

'Farewell, *Tuló*,' Amelie whispered, 'even though we don't say goodbyes anymore.' She closed her eyes and gripped the little piece of crystal in her pocket, remembering the very first night Isla came to stay: *The New Hope* they'd watched together; the shooting star they'd all seen, and the wishes they'd made. There would surely be many new hopes still to come, and shooting stars, and wishes too. But for now there was much to be done. No-time-to-lose!

Without a word, Tim and Isla slipped away, leaving Amelie alone at her little desk. Somehow though she knew she would never be really alone; for there at her shoulder were Dorin and the Commander, and now her father too. A whole family of Earth Watchers, urging her on! She picked up her favourite pen, the one with the rainbow ink, and with a sense of great urgency, began to write:

'The Earth Watchers' – a true story by Amelie Joan Trott
Chapter One

Author's Note

Dear Reader,

When I began to write this book I had no idea that it would somehow be linked with the appearance on the world stage of a now very famous young person. In August 2018, Greta Thunberg, a fifteen year old Swedish Climate Activist, bravely began her first Fridays for Future strike. Curiously, that very same week, on a laptop somewhere in England, Amelie Trott, aged ten years and eleven months, was appealing to young people around the world to form an enormous Human Shield to prevent weapons of destruction from ever being used again.

Thus the real and the fictional girls became leaders in a fight to save the planet, and all because the adults of the world could no longer be trusted to safeguard their future.

I truly hope they have both inspired you and given you hope for the future. Meanwhile, our friends the Earth Watchers have asked me to leave you with this final message:

'Greetings, we salute you!

Perhaps, like Amelie, Tim and Isla, you too have a cherished ambition – something you'd like to achieve one day. As you know, Amelie dreamed of being a best-selling author, even though she was pretty hopeless at school. But did she let that stop her? Of course not! And it didn't stop there. You see, we invited her to tell a more remarkable story still – about us, the Earth Watchers, and how children can change the world for the better.

So, whatever *your* dream may be, however seemingly

small or insignificant, always believe in it. *See* it working out, *feel* it happening, and above all, *never give up!*

And don't forget this: whatever you try to do to help others will be championed by us, the Forces of Light – we shall always be there to cheer you on your way! For just like Amelie, Tim and Isla, *you* are the hero of a very big story indeed, and you already have all it takes to make your world a better place.

So, please remember our challenge and the important part you have to play! *It is down to you now, Children of Luga!'*

Moyra Irving
March 2020

Glossary

Earth Watchers – a group of advanced individuals from other planets

Madagascar - an island off the coast of East Africa whose capital city is Antananarivo

FIFA – International Federation of Association Football

Hornby Dublo – a British model railway brand

Merci – *(French)* Thank you

Gateaux - *(French)* Cakes

Au revoir - *(French)* Goodbye

Taffeta - a fine fabric used for special gowns

Dengue (pronounced *denguee*) **fever** – a viral infection spread by mosquitoes

ATA – Air Transport Auxiliary (female pilot in World War 2)

Tiger Moth – a 1930s biplane used by the RAF for training

Spitfire – a British fighter aircraft used before, during, and after World War 2

Arthur Mee's Children's Encyclopaedias – first published in 1910

Mills and Boon – a British publisher of romance novels

Pas de problème - *(French)* No problem

Tuló – a title given to an Earth Watcher of high rank; a Commander

Oh, my giddy aunt! – a popular, old-fashioned saying used to denote surprise

Dumela – *(South African)* Hello

Kom snel! – *(Dutch)* Come quickly!

Raadhuis – *(Dutch)* Town Hall

Hayaku kite! – *(Japanese)* Come quickly!

Scan the QR code for Teaching Materials and Activity Sheets
https://dixibooks.com/categories/childrens-books/amelie_trott/